One O'Clock Hustle

One O'Clock Hustle

A Rebecca Mayfield Mystery

JOANNE PENCE

QUAIL HILL PUBLISHING

Quail Hill Publishing
PO Box 64
Eagle, ID 83616

Visit our website at www.quailhillpublishing.net

First Quail Hill Publishing Paperback Printing: April 2014
First Quail Hill Publishing E-book: April 2014

ISBN-13: 978-0615992914
ISBN-10: 0615992919

To Aaron and Zach

Chapter 1

A T 1:05 A.M. ON Sunday morning, after working twenty-four hours straight on the capture of an armed suspect in the murder of a liquor store clerk, Inspector Rebecca Mayfield sat alone at her desk in Homicide.

She was exhausted. But just as she finished writing up her notes on the tension-filled arrest, ready to head home for some much-needed sleep, the police dispatcher called: a shooting, one fatality, reported at Big Caesar's Nightclub.

Rebecca had heard of the club, located in San Francisco's touristy North Beach area. She was the first investigator to arrive at the scene, and flashed her badge at the uniformed police officer at the door. "Mayfield. Homicide."

"Good news," Officer Danzig said, all but beaming. "We're holding the killer. The bouncers caught him. He clammed up right away, but you'll find him in the manager's office."

Rebecca's eyebrows rose. She had never had witnesses capture the suspect before. "Interesting. And good; very good." Maybe she would get some sleep tonight after all.

"His name is ..." the officer pulled out his notepad and read from it, "Richard Amalfi."

Rebecca was suddenly jolted wide awake. "What did you say?"

"Richard Amalfi. He's well known at the club, apparently comes here frequently. Everyone calls him Richie."

It can't be. Her mouth went dry. "I see." There are a lot of Amalfis in this city, she told herself. "Did you see him?"

"I did. Not quite six feet, medium build, black hair, late thirties or early forties."

Damn. That sounded like the Richie Amalfi she knew. He was quite a character to be sure, but a murderer? The thought jarred her. She shook her head, needing to focus on the crime, on doing her job. "What do we know about the victim?"

"No name yet. Female, in her thirties, I'd say. We only know she was a customer. Apparently she came in with the man who killed her."

"Allegedly killed her," Rebecca automatically added.

"Allegedly," Danzig repeated. "Although they said he was caught in the act. The body's in the bookkeeper's office."

Caught in the act ... The words reverberated round and round in her head as she tried to listen to a run-down of the club's layout—the ballroom straight ahead, the coat closet and restrooms to the left, and beyond them, cordoned off with yellow tape, the corridor with the manager's office where Richie was being held, and the bookkeeper's office where the murder took place.

"Was the victim connected to the bookkeeper in some way?" she asked.

"No one has said. The bookkeeper isn't here this time of night."

Rebecca would have been shocked if he was. Nine-to-fivers liked their beauty sleep.

Danzig went on to assure her that he and his partner

had immediately shut down the club and no one had been allowed to enter or leave.

She thanked the officer and stepped away from him, drawing a deep breath as she thought of all that was to come.

If Homicide were a family, Richie Amalfi would be a close relative. Rebecca's favorite co-worker, Inspector Paavo Smith, was engaged to Richie's cousin, Angelina Amalfi.

From Paavo, she knew Richie could come up with just about anything that anyone might want. Need something big, small, expensive, cheap, common, or rare? It didn't matter. Cousin Richie could provide. Many people seemed to "know a guy who knows a guy." Well, Richie was that guy— the one people went to when they needed something. She didn't want to get into what that "something" might be, or the legality of how he got it. But that didn't make him a killer ... she hoped.

She entered the elegant ballroom with white cloth-covered tables forming a semi-circle around an empty dance floor. She had never been there before—beer and pizza were her speed; jeans, turtleneck sweaters, black leather jackets, and boots her style.

The popular nightspot had been designed to look like a glamorous nightclub from the forties, the sort of place where Sinatra, Tony Bennett or Dean Martin might have sung, where women dressed in glittery gowns, men wore black or white jackets with bow ties, and "dancing cheek-to-cheek" referred to the couple's faces, not other parts of the anatomy. No hip-hop, rap or, God-forbid, country-western would ever be performed at Big Caesar's.

She could absolutely see Richie in a place like this—as absolutely as she couldn't see him killing anyone. Yet he was "caught in the act," the police officer had said.

As much as she didn't want to believe it, she needed to

put aside her personal feelings. She had no more reason to believe he was innocent than she did anyone else accused of a crime. And yet ...

And yet, she couldn't help but remember the day, last Christmas Eve, when she worked alone in Homicide and he came in looking for Paavo for help with a problem. Paavo was off duty, so she ended up helping, and had spent the day and well into the night with him, finally heading home in the early hours of Christmas morning. Their time together hadn't been long, but it had been intense, including chases and shootouts, and the kind of life and death struggles— crazy though they were—that left emotions raw and defenses down. To her amazement, she had enjoyed being with him.

She then used the next several days wondering if she'd been stupid to have spent so much time with him.

Not that anything had "happened" between them. Heaven forbid! After all, from the moment she first met him, she knew he wasn't her type, and he clearly realized the same about her. Still, from time to time, she couldn't help but wonder ...

In any case, he never contacted her again—which told her that the only thing stupid was to have wasted any time whatsoever thinking about him. Of course, if he had called and asked her out, she would have refused to go. She wondered if he hadn't realized that. He was, she had discovered, curiously perceptive.

The band now jauntily played *"The Best is Yet to Come,"* but a sullen, wary mood blanketed the room.

When she left the ballroom, she found that her partner, Bill Sutter, had arrived. He was taking statements from the bouncers. Rebecca walked around to get a quick feel for the nightclub's layout and exits, both doors and windows.

Despite wanting to see and question Richie, she would

save him for last.

From her several years of experience in Homicide, she knew that the more she learned about a situation the better her first questions would be, and the better she could judge the veracity of a suspect's answers. Since she knew the alleged "perp," she was going to have to be even more by-the-book in this case than she normally was.

She ducked under the yellow crime scene tape. A cop stood at the door of one of the offices.

"Homicide," Rebecca said as she put on latex gloves and entered the office. The victim lay face up in the center of the room.

She appeared to be in her early thirties and to Rebecca's eye the sort of blonde—beautiful, slim, and expensively dressed—that fit easily in a classy place like Big Caesar's; the sort of woman she could imagine Richie going out with.

A gunshot had struck her heart. Death was most likely instantaneous or close to it. Blood soaked the carpet beneath her.

Rebecca surveyed the rest of the room. The window was open wide, bringing in blustery, cold air. Piles of papers lay in a wind-tossed jumble across the desk where a brass nameplate read "Daniel Pasternak." Behind it hung a sappy Thomas Kincaid painting of little sparkling pastel-colored cottages ready-made for Disney's seven dwarfs. On the floor near the body lay a small satin handbag.

Rebecca picked it up and opened it. The bag was empty except for two twenties and a lipstick. No cell phone; no credit cards. That was surprising, and odd.

Just then, the medical examiner, Evelyn Ramirez, arrived. She wore a red sequined blouse, black silk slacks, and diamonds. Her black hair was pulled back tight and pinned up in a sleek chignon. She had obviously been called away from some big shindig and intended to return to it soon.

The ME quickly took in the body and its surroundings. "Well, this'll be fast."

Rebecca watched Ramirez do the preliminary examination to make sure no big surprises turned up—such as the corpse had actually been dead for twelve hours before someone found her, not twenty seconds like everyone said. The entry wound indicated the shot had been fired at close range, a few feet away, which was consistent with the killer and victim being together in the room.

With the exam concluded, the time had come for Rebecca to face Richie.

She took a deep breath and opened the door to the office of the nightclub manager.

Richie stood at the window, his back to her, looking into the night. His wrists were handcuffed behind him.

Two cops sat near the desk—a desk overflowing with paperwork. When Rebecca entered, they walked over to the door and stood beside it.

Richie slowly turned and faced her. Even in handcuffs he seemed calm, cool, and suave in a black jacket, white shirt, and black bow tie, almost like something out of a James Bond movie. Or, more in keeping with him and his friends, *The Godfather*.

"Richie Amalfi," she whispered.

He took a step towards her, then stopped, his deep-set, heavy-lidded brown eyes troubled and questioning. As he gazed at her, she saw something else in them, but she wasn't sure what.

She steeled herself and raised her head high, giving him a cold, icy stare.

His shoulders seemed to sag at that. "Rebecca

Rulebook," he murmured, then pushed a noisy breath past his lips, and wryly shook his head. "Guess I should kiss my ass good-bye."

His saying that, his thinking that way about her, momentarily stung, but she pushed the feelings aside and concentrated on the job before her. She pulled out a chair for Richie, and then another for herself facing it. Truth be told, she moved the furniture around to give herself time to think, and to give her breathing a chance to return to normal.

"Have a seat, Richie." She prided herself on being a cop. Raised in Idaho, she had always followed the straight and narrow, and believed that all God's children were created equally. But if one of them got out of line, the full power of the law should stomp down until they saw the light. And Richie Amalfi was no exception.

"Look, Rebecca—"

"Inspector Mayfield," she said harshly, too harshly. She sat in the chair she had provided for herself and waited. She knew the rumors that he was "connected." She hadn't wanted to believe there was anything bad about him, but if he did kill someone in her city, on her watch, she didn't give a damn about those connections or family ties—current or future.

He sat facing her. "I didn't kill Meaghan Blakely." He leaned towards her as he spoke, his gaze intense, his voice earnest. "I found her body, that's all."

Thank you, she thought. He had just identified the victim. She ignored his protestation of innocence. All suspects did that.

"Tell me about Meaghan Blakely. Where does she live?"

"I don't know. I just met her." He started to stand, then changed his mind and remained seated. She could sense his tension, his need to fidget—he constantly fidgeted that one day they spent together. It drove her crazy.

Just then, Bill Sutter walked into the room.

Rebecca's partner was a burden to her. She knew from watching the other homicide inspectors that loyalty to one's partner was important, so she never complained no matter how furious he made her.

"Never-Take-A-Chance" Sutter was in his late fifties, about six feet tall, slim, with short steel gray hair, a long face, multiple bags under watery gray eyes, and thin, constantly down-turned colorless lips. He had been in Homicide so long he could have doubled as a walking, talking history book. Unfortunately, he had lost interest in the job and focused more on his retirement than his day-to-day duties. He talked about it all the time, and obsessed with worry that, like a character in a movie he once saw, he might be killed in the line of duty before his retirement day arrived. As a result, he did all he could to avoid putting himself in any danger—a difficult task when confronting killers.

Richie and Sutter eyed each other warily. Richie stiffened.

"Please continue," Rebecca said.

Squaring his shoulders as best he could with his hands cuffed, Richie stated, "I'm not saying another word until I talk to my lawyer!"

Sutter folded his arms and with a scowl faced Rebecca. "As far as I'm concerned, that does it for him. He wants to lawyer up, fine. I've got two witnesses' statements that he held the murder weapon and was trying to escape out the window when they caught him. I say we take him down to the station. If we can't question him, we book him."

A part of her wanted to believe Richie was innocent, but the evidence told her otherwise and she was too tired to try to argue against it, especially since Richie had no interest in cooperating. "You're right," she said finally.

Sutter nodded. "Good. Look, I'll handle everything. Go home, get some sleep. We've been at work non-stop since yesterday afternoon. We'll have clearer heads tomorrow."

At Sutter's mention of sleep, all the fatigue she had tried to ignore struck and the quiet throbbing of her head became an insistent drumbeat. She nodded. Without allowing herself to look back at Richie one last time, sick at heart, she left the room.

Chapter 2

THE LIGHT OF DAWN filled the eastern sky before Rebecca reached the alleyway where her tiny apartment was located. When she first arrived in the city, in search of excitement, romance, money—all the things small-town singles think of when they decide to leave home and go off on their own—she gravitated towards the streets and alleyways on the hillside just above the seedy Tenderloin, the area she had read about in Dashiell Hammett's *The Maltese Falcon*.

She found a small in-law apartment in a narrow, dead-end street off of Taylor called Mulford Alley. In San Francisco, Rebecca learned that "in-law" meant illegal, built against zoning restrictions, and most likely built without permits. At first, the idea of living in an illegal apartment bothered her, until she learned they existed all over the city and she would not be the only cop who lived in one.

Her three-story building consisted of two flats over a ground-level garage and storage room. Her apartment had once been that storage space. Rebecca especially liked its privacy. To reach it, you had to go through a door that seemed as if it would open into the garage. Instead, it led to a breezeway to the back yard. The front door to her two-room dwelling faced that yard.

The landlord kept flowers and herbs in planter boxes and pots in the yard year round. Sometimes, if she focused hard on a group of flowers, a cluster of pink and white hydrangeas for example, she could almost forget some of the horrors she saw on the job.

She had a love-hate relationship with the city and her work. Sometimes, she wanted to throw up her hands and quit in frustration at the bureaucratic minutia that got in her way. And other times, such as when she returned to her snug little apartment after successfully investigating a murder, she was amazed and grateful that her job—her life—could be both interesting and rewarding.

Another perk to her apartment's location was free, on-street parking. To find any parking space in San Francisco took perseverance and more luck than most people had. In Mulford Alley, the city had painted the sidewalk curb on one side of the narrow street red so cars wouldn't park there. Others who lived in the alley told Rebecca that if she parked up on the sidewalk, atop the red, she wouldn't be ticketed. Meter maids never bothered to enter it. That bit of "law-breaking" also took her a while to get used to—another "everyone does it in San Francisco" sort of crime.

Earlier that night, after leaving Richie with Bill Sutter, she had gone into the ballroom to deal with the customers. There, she met the club manager, Harrison Sidwell, a tall, thin man with dyed black hair, a mustache, black-framed glasses, and pin-prick brown eyes.

She talked to the policemen who had taken everyone's name and contact information along with statements that not one of them had seen anything, and she then let the patrons leave. They hurried from the building, heads high, complaints loud, a few even daring to swear under their breaths at the uniformed officers.

Rebecca watched them go, then, dead tired, she took a statement from Sidwell covering all he had seen and heard, plus obtained from him the bookkeeper's full name, address and phone number. Perhaps the bookkeeper knew why the dead woman was in his office; no one else knew, and if Richie Amalfi knew, he wasn't saying.

After that, she returned to Homicide to run a few quick checks on the name Meaghan Blakely. She could find no record of any kind under that name, not even using alternative spellings.

Finally, she headed home.

The case troubled her for a number of reasons, not the least being Richie's involvement. But before spending any more time investigating, she needed some sleep.

If she had been tired before she went to Big Caesar's last night, it was nothing compared to the bone-aching weariness that consumed her now. Her eyes felt as if the entire Sahara had settled in them, and her headache caused shooting pains that rattled her teeth.

After parking in her usual red zone, she stumbled towards the brown and tan stucco building she called home. She paused, not because of any sound, but the feeling that someone watched her. That someone was near. As she spun around, she unzipped her Galco holster handbag in case she needed to use her Glock. Normally, she carried her weapon in a middle-of-the-back holster, but it jabbed her when she drove. Tonight, she was too tired to put up with the discomfort and removed it. Besides, she was only going home.

She scanned the street, glowing golden and hazy with early morning mist. Nothing moved. No cars, no people, no pigeons or seagulls, not even a piece of trash buffeted about by the ever-present bay breeze.

Nothing but nerves and exhaustion, she told herself. She rezipped the gun compartment of her handbag, and took out her keys. Perhaps she had seen too much death this weekend.

With eyes that scarcely had the strength to stay open, she found the lock in the door beside the garage, slipped in the key and pushed the door open. A hand clamped over her mouth, another around her waist and she felt herself dragged into the breezeway. The attacker didn't lift her—at five foot ten, it would take Shaquille O'Neal to lift her off her feet—and judging from the feel of the body against hers, he was about her height.

She struggled to break his hold, and as she did, she caught a glimpse of a black onyx and gold cuff link. She recognized it. Fury replaced fear and she stomped down hard on the man's foot.

"God damn, Rebecca!" Her would-be captor let her go as he hopped on one foot. "I just wanted to make sure you wouldn't scream and wake the neighbors!"

"Richie!" She couldn't believe it. When she last saw him, Bill Sutter was leading him out to the patrol car for the ride to city jail. "I never scream."

"I don't want you to shoot me either." He grabbed her shoulder bag. "I know this is where you've got your gun."

"What are you doing here?" she demanded as they played tug-of-war with her purse. He curled himself around it like a running back bracing to be tackled. "How did your lawyer get you released already?"

"I've got to talk to you about that." He looked from side to side, even at the roof, as if expecting a SWAT team to rappel into her garden. "I don't want you to go arresting me before I've had a chance to speak my piece."

"Let go of my handbag first!"

He did. She placed it back on her shoulder and then folded her arms, still glaring. "You've already been arrested."

"Is there someplace warm we can go talk?" he asked, rubbing his arms. "I've been freezing my ass off out here waiting for you to come home. Where the hell have you been all this time?"

"You've been here all night?" His words made no sense to her. Even a quick release after booking took time, and his case involved murder.

"I asked the cop who was walking me to the squad car to loosen the handcuffs and then ... I don't know what happened. Something came over me, I guess. Or maybe the cop and Sutter tripped, because they were suddenly on the ground, and so I ran. Luckily, I'd left my car down by Sakura Gardens. I got out of the area easily except for one problem." He held up his left wrist. One end of the handcuffs was still attached to it, and dangling down, the other end of the cuffs was wide open. Then his head cocked slightly as he studied her. "You mean Sutter didn't tell you?"

Sutter! She could imagine that he didn't want to tell his partner that he'd managed to lose their main suspect. Suspect, hell! He had two eyewitnesses, and from all she'd heard and seen, enough evidence to incriminate a saint. And Richie Amalfi was no saint.

But something--call it "cop sense" or whatever--told her he was innocent. And now, for some weird reason, he came here to her. She wanted to know why. Also, the more she thought about it, the more pissed off she became at Sutter. Why didn't he tell her immediately what had happened? Everything was so crazy, and she was so tired—and cold—she decided to take Amalfi up on his request. "We'll go to my apartment," she said through gritted teeth. "My house keys must still be in the breezeway door lock."

He held out her keys, dangling them by the NRA medallion on her key chain. He glanced at it. "You are one bad-ass broad."

She grabbed the keys, shut and locked the door to the breezeway, and then marched to her apartment door and unlocked it. "Get inside, and don't try anything funny."

"Yes, Inspector," he said with a grin.

For a moment, he thought she had unlocked the wrong door. The apartment was nothing like the gun-toting, NRA-joining, leather-wearing, karate-chopping, baton-wielding super cop he knew she was. He even heard she could watch autopsies and not flinch.

Guys on the force called her the Iron Maiden, and from their comments, they weren't only talking about her prowess as a cop.

Yet the homey, old-fashioned apartment reminded him of a country cabin. Quilts and throws in varying combinations of red, blue, and green ginghams, checks and plaids covered mismatched furniture, probably from second-hand stores. Ruffle-edged pillows looked comfortable and inviting. From the front door, he could see the whole apartment, a living room with a small kitchen area in one corner, and a bedroom with a queen-sized bed (hmm, what was the lady not telling?) piled high with a fluffy down comforter and more pillows.

He took a couple of steps into the room and then froze at the sound of a low, deep growl.

On a red satin pillow stood the silliest looking dog he had ever seen. Smaller than most cats, it was furless except for a tuft of hair pulled up into a blue ribbon on the very top of its head. Its eyes could have been big brown jawbreakers.

"What in the hell is *that*?" he asked.

The mutt barked at him then ran to Rebecca and stood on its back legs, its front paws against her knee, wagging its tail and begging to be lifted.

She scooped it up. "You're right to bark, Spike," she said, cuddling the beast as she carried him to the kitchen area. "He's a bad man."

Spike?

"This is just a temporary reprieve," Rebecca said to Richie as she dished barely more than a tablespoon of Alpo into a bowl. "I have to take you back, you know."

"I didn't do it, Rebecca—"

"Inspector Mayfield!" she reminded him. The dog began eating as she turned on the heater.

"Inspector," he repeated. "I don't know if what happened to me was just dumb luck or if I've been set up, but I didn't do it. And you know I'm telling you the truth."

"Hah!"

He couldn't stop himself from shivering from the cold and more—as if the tense, rigid way he had held himself while waiting for her, wondering what else to do, where else to go, could no longer be maintained.

She must have seen him shiver because she grabbed one of the afghan throws on the sofa and put it over his shoulders. "Sit on the rocking chair by the vent." She pointed to a maple rocker with green plaid seat and back pads, held in place by large matching bows. "You'll warm up faster so we can get you to City Jail. Coffee or tea?"

"Coffee, please. Look, I know you believe me. You're a good cop. If you thought there was any chance at all I was guilty, no way you'd let me into your apartment. You'd whisk me off to stir so fast it'd make my head spin. But you didn't."

"Don't push your luck, Richie. It might just be that you

looked like a whipped puppy outside."

He shook his head and moved to the spot she suggested. Immediately, he felt warm air on his feet and ankles. He hadn't even realized how frozen his feet had become. He could have stayed warm if he remained in his car, but then he would have missed her. He had parked far from Mulford Alley, on a street she most likely wouldn't pass as she went home. She knew his car, a black Porsche, and even though this city had a fair number of similar cars, if she noticed a car like his nearby, she might become suspicious.

So, he parked six blocks away, walked to her building, hid in nearby doorway, and waited for her to show up. He had become so cold and miserable, he wondered if it had been a mistake not to stay in jail and take his chances with the law.

But he had overheard Bill Sutter and the cop talking, and their conversation convinced him just how dumb that would be.

He could have tried to run fast and far, but the cops surely had put an APB out on his car within a matter of minutes of him taking off. Besides, where would he go? And if he ran, he would look guilty—even guiltier than he did by his escape.

On top of all that, the real killer had to be laying low somewhere in San Francisco laughing his head off that Richie would take the rap for him. Whoever that *figlio di puttana* was, he wouldn't get away with it.

He would find the bastard who did this, and prove to the world that he—Richard Joseph Francis Amalfi—was innocent.

Somehow.

Then he thought of Rebecca. Oh, pardon—*Inspector Mayfield*. If anyone could do it, she could.

He hoped.

He watched her as she took off her jacket and then moved around the kitchen making coffee. She was tall, and if he wasn't so worried about his situation, he could appreciate being here with her—in fact, he could appreciate everything about her. Her looks were off-beat, yet he considered her as close to gorgeous as any woman had the right to be, and she didn't seem to have any idea of it. She usually twisted her blond hair back and held it in place with a big barrette, as if she didn't know what long, lush hair like hers could do to a man. Her face was kind of triangle shaped, with a pointed, stubborn chin. Her lips were full, but her eyes really got to him. They were big and blue. He had always been a sucker for eyes like hers.

She handed him a mug of black coffee, breaking off his wayward thoughts. He knew she wasn't the type of woman he should ever think about that way. He turned his focus back to himself and his predicament while taking a sip of coffee. To his surprise, it had bourbon in it. "Isn't it against the rules to ply the suspects with liquor, Inspector?" he asked.

"Consider it medicinal," she said.

"Are you having some, too?" he asked.

"Not on your life. I have the feeling I'm going to need all my senses to deal with you." She sat on the sofa, holding her coffee mug, and said, "Now, let's start at the beginning."

Richie shut his eyes a moment, then spoke. "I went to the races this afternoon, Golden Gate Fields. At the Turf Club, I saw Meaghan Blakely. She smiled, and we started talking. We hit it off. I asked her to dinner."

"Did you pick her up at her home?" Rebecca asked.

"No. She said she'd meet me at the restaurant. We went to Sakura Gardens down the street, and from there, we walked over to Big Caesar's. Believe me, I never touched her! Why would I kill her? I'm a witness!"

Rebecca plowed on. "Did she mention family, friends?"

He gazed heavenward, as if for patience. "She claimed to be fairly new in town from L.A."

"Then what?"

Richie slumped back in the chair with a scowl. "After a couple drinks, she excused herself to go to the ladies' room. A few minutes later, some guy, a really big guy, slipped me an envelope. Inside was a note from Danny Pasternak saying he wanted to see me immediately, so I went."

"He's the club bookkeeper?"

Richie hesitated, then said, "Well ... yeah, you could say that."

"Weren't you surprised to get a note from him?"

Richie tugged at his ear, then looked from one wall to another. "Not really. We're old friends. We go way back."

She frowned. "Weren't you surprised he was working so late at night?"

"It's Saturday night!"

"So?"

He shrugged.

She pursed her lips. "Why did he want to see you?"

"I never found out. When I reached his office, I knocked, then opened the door and walked in. Instead of seeing Danny sitting at his desk, I saw Meaghan on the floor." He seemed to shudder from the memory, and then ran his hand over the back of his head.

She waited.

"From the corner of my eye," he began, "I saw something move. I spun around to see this guy with a gun. A big mother ... uh, guy. He wore a ski mask. I lunged at him, grabbing for the gun. It went off."

"Were you or this other man hit?"

"I don't think so. I froze at the sound. I didn't feel anything, but I remembered guys who'd been shot telling me they didn't feel pain for a long time, only cold, horrible cold." He went a bit pale at the thought, then cleared his throat. "Anyway, as I was saying, the shooter, the *real* shooter shoved me hard, and I fell over. The shooter went out the window. I picked up the gun—"

"You picked up the gun? You got it away from him, then?" she asked.

"Yeah, I must have."

"Why pick it up? Why not leave it?"

"I was going after the killer! I wanted to stop him, and I didn't think he'd respond to, 'Stop, pretty please.'"

She shook her head. "Go on."

"Like I said, I picked up the gun and ran to the window to go after the guy. Then I heard some people screaming behind me." Richie paused as if reliving the scene. His dark eyes met Rebecca's. "All I remember are screams, lots of screams. The bouncers came running into the room, and yelled at me to put down the gun. I tried to tell them I didn't do it, that the shooter went out the window. No one listened. Instead, they hustled me into an office."

"The bouncers claimed they kept an eye on Pasternak's office, and that no one went in there all night except the woman and you. They said Pasternak wasn't even here."

"They're wrong! The waiter, or whoever he was, gave me a note from him!"

"Where is the note?" Rebecca asked.

Richie's gaze went to his jacket pockets, then the floor as if trying to remember. "I'm pretty sure I left it on the table.

Meaghan's coat—full-length, black, probably cashmere—was there, plus our martinis. The note was from Danny. I swear!"

Rebecca nodded. "We'll look for it. In any case, the bouncers told my partner a gunshot come from the room, and when they ran in, they saw you with the gun trying to climb out the window. They wrestled you down, took the gun, and called us."

"So? I already told you what happened. While you two waste time on me, the killer's probably half-way to Argentina!"

Richie told a good story, Rebecca thought, one that would explain how the gun ended up with his fingerprints on it, and why he would have gunpowder residue on his hand when they tested it. There was just one problem. She didn't see any extraneous bullet holes in the victim or the office, and only one shell lay on the floor from the gun.

No one heard two shots—and they would have if Richie's claim were true that he found Blakely shot to death and that the gun had been fired a second time as he fought with the 'real' killer.

Richie wanted her to believe that the killer managed to shoot Blakely, and then retrieved the shell from the gunshot—a shot no one heard. But if he had the presence of mind to pick up a shell, why didn't he shoot Richie as soon as he walked in? If he had already killed one person, what stopped him from killing a second?

She quickly phoned the head of the Crime Scene Investigation team. He and his team were still at the night club looking for evidence, and would be there many hours more. She asked him to let her know immediately if his team found a second bullet hole and shell, and then she asked if he would locate the table Richie and Meaghan had shared.

He did, and saw Meaghan's black cashmere coat and two

half-empty cocktail glasses at a table, but he found no note from Danny Pasternak.

She thanked him and hung up.

Richie had given her a good story about some other person shooting the woman and escaping out the window, except that no one saw anyone else enter Pasternak's office and the bouncers claimed to have run into the room within seconds of hearing a shot fired.

Why, then, did she believe him?

One thing she knew was true: he appeared exhausted and so was she. Even thinking about dragging him back down to City Jail was a chore. She knew she could do it, but for some reason, she didn't want to.

Her phone rang.

She stood and took her cell phone from her jeans pocket. It was Sutter. "What's happening?"

She paced, growing increasingly irritated as a chagrined Sutter admitted their prisoner had escaped, that he'd been searching for him with the cops and that's why he hadn't called sooner.

Yeah, right. "Well, guess what," she began when she felt a tap on her shoulder.

Richie pointed her own gun at her. Her eyes narrowed as they went from the gun to him. He shook his head and gestured for her to hang up.

She knew she was safe with him, and knew she could take him if she had to. She pushed his arm so that the gun was no longer pointing at her, and continued her conversation. "Okay, Bill, keep looking. Let me know how things progress." She listened to a few more words, then hung up.

"I do not believe you." Rebecca's voice dripped with disgust.

He handed the gun back to her. "Okay, so I wouldn't have shot you," he said. "But you've got to admit, being threatened made it easier for you not to tell Sutter I was here, no?"

"No!" She folded her arms. Well, maybe so, she thought. "Why are you here, Richie? And how do you know where I live?"

He shrugged, then took off his skewed bowtie, dropped it onto the coffee table, and unbuttoned his collar. The afghan she had placed over his shoulders now lay on the chair by the heater with Spike atop it.

"I thought about you a lot after that day." He seemed to study her as he spoke. "You remember the one?"

She nodded. Christmas Eve. How could she forget it?

"I thought, maybe if I waited a while, I'd ask you out, you know. So I asked around, and learned where you lived. That's all."

She nodded again, then rubbed her aching forehead. Obviously, he had thought better of asking her out, for which she was grateful. She might have felt bad about refusing to see him if he had called. Now, she had no reason for guilt whatsoever.

"As I said, why are you here?"

"If anybody can prove me innocent and find Meaghan's killer, it's you," he stated bluntly.

"Me? You're joking! Why not go to Paavo? He's engaged to your cousin, almost part of the family."

"That's why. Anything he does would be suspect, and it would make him suspect as well. I don't want to do anything that could mess up him and Cousin Angie."

"But messing up my career is just fine?"

"I trust you."

That stopped her.

"I trust you," he continued, his voice every bit as buttery smooth and oddly seductive as she remembered it. "I trust you to get to the bottom of this, to find out the truth. I saw the man who killed Meaghan. Not his face, but his height, the way he held himself, the way he moved. I want the bastard caught, but I can't do that if I'm sitting in jail."

Clearly, the only reason she bothered to listen to him, or found him in any way convincing, was that she was too tired to think straight.

"Look," Richie continued, "you're ready to drop. Get some sleep. I'll be right here when you wake up."

"But ..." She glanced at her watch. She'd been awake more hours than she could count at the moment. Between dead bodies and Richie, it felt like a hundred. She sat on the sofa while he moved Spike and the blanket onto the floor.

"Look at it this way," he offered, his tone soft and soothing. "Where would I go? If I wanted to run, I would already be far from here. But I don't want that. So get some sleep. Maybe I will too."

He took off his jacket and then sat on the chair, resting his head back against it.

She waited for him to shut his eyes, but he didn't. Instead, she found herself nodding off. She tried to shake off the sleepiness, but the heater's warmth seemed to creep over her, soothing and restful. Spike jumped onto her lap, lay down, and soon snored softly.

As if with a will of their own, her long legs stretched out on the cushions and she slid down a bit on the seats. In a goofy way, Richie's words made sense, and a ten-minute power nap was tempting. She wouldn't let herself do it, however. Only in the interest of comfort did she turn onto her side and lay her head against the armrest while, as Spike scrambled to find a new comfortable spot, she heard herself murmur, "No way would I go to sleep with you here, Richie Amalfi."

Chapter 3

REBECCA OPENED HER eyes to see her bedroom filled with sunlight. *What? How can that...*

She lay on her back atop her bed, fully dressed, the comforter over her. She didn't even remember going into the bedroom last night.

She felt something binding her right wrist. She turned her head ... and bolted straight up to a sitting position.

Richie Amalfi lay next to her, fast asleep.

Her gaze immediately dropped to her wrist, and she received another shock. Her right wrist was cuffed to his left.

Handcuffs?

He had handcuffed *her* to *him*?

How could she have let herself to fall asleep with him in her apartment? Why did she allow herself to act so foolishly in his presence? What was wrong with her?

The world flashed red as pure, unharnessed fury washed over her. It was all his fault! How could he have such nerve, such chutzpah, such moxie, as to handcuff her and then lie down on her bed?

She would kill him. That's all there was to it. If a firing squad was legal in the state she'd gladly pull a trigger. If electric chairs were still used, she'd throw the switch. She'd sharpen the blade on a guillotine ... or dull it. She wasn't fussy.

She glared at him. The area below his eyes had darkened from fatigue, and his brow furrowed as if from worry even in sleep. Yet, the way his black hair flopped onto his forehead gave him a disarmingly innocent look.

Richie Amalfi innocent? Hah!

Still, she wondered how anyone so rotten could look so angelic when sleeping.

Fortunately, she sat on the side of the bed where she usually slept—the side where she kept a gun under the mattress. Lots of cops slept that way. The middle of the night, when asleep, was a cop's most vulnerable time. Moving slowly, she slid her left hand between the mattress and box spring. She couldn't find the gun. Awkwardly, she reached a little further. It was missing.

He had to have taken it. Damn him! Loading him into a wood chipper was too good for him.

Now, as her head cleared, she had a vague memory of him helping her pull off her boots and guiding her towards the bedroom, of her arguing against it, but being so tired she all but fell onto the mattress.

She lay back down again and flung her left arm over her forehead. She thought about getting her handcuff key and freeing herself, but then a very different idea came to mind.

She wondered exactly what had gone through that crime-infested mind of his last night. Why, of all the people he knew, of all the places he could have run to, did he come here to her? The excuse he gave made sense and flattered, she must admit. But there had to be more to it than that.

Amalfi learned fast, and between friends, relatives, and his own, probably bad, experiences, he knew far too much about police procedures. Coming here, he clearly had something up his sleeve. He always did. And once he got what he wanted, he'd take off and disappear again.

Most crooks and killers she could take down with no problem. But then, most crooks and even killers were pretty dumb. She couldn't say that about Richie. He could play dumb, but he wasn't. From everything she had heard about him from Paavo Smith, and from her own limited experience with him, he very likely had something in mind, and she wanted to know what it was.

A way to do it came to her—a plan that wouldn't exactly be easy to pull off. Was she a good enough actress? And, most importantly, did she dare do it?

Yes, as a matter of fact, she did. Two could play at his little game!

Was he still asleep? He no longer breathed deeply, and he hadn't snored at all. What kind of a man didn't snore or at least breathe heavily as he slept?

She believed he faked sleep at this point. Maybe curiosity over her motives gripped him, just as she was curious about his. She glanced at the small lamp on the nightstand beside her. He would soon find out exactly how she felt.

She yanked the lamp's plug from the wall.

Tightly clutching the base of the lamp, she lifted and held it over his head as if ready to let it drop.

His arm reached out and grabbed hers. "Good morning to you, too," he grumbled. "Do you always wake up in such a good mood?"

She sat up again. "Who the hell do you think you are?"

He sat up as well, removed the offending lamp from her hand, and dropped it between them on the bed.

"What's the reason for this?" she demanded, wriggling her manacled wrist.

"You might have had second thoughts." He rubbed his eyes and yawned. "How the hell was I supposed to know what might go through that cop brain of yours? You might have run out, called somebody, maybe shot me in my sleep. I wouldn't put it past you!"

"You were right about the last one," she muttered.

It struck her that she was having a conversation with a man she hardly knew, a possible murderer, while sitting on her bed. At this point she didn't know if she were angrier at Richie or at herself for going along with this farce. She got off the bed, stretching out her arm as she did so. "Now, wise guy, how are you going to get these cuffs off, short of going to a police station? I want to use the bathroom, and I'll be damned if you're coming with me. You get this off me, or I'll take an ax to you!"

"Calm down, Inspector," Richie said as he crawled over the bed to her side and also got off it. "I need some coffee." His slacks were badly rumpled, his white dress shirt wrinkled and unbuttoned at the neck, and he needed a shave. He looked like hell.

"Listen, Amalfi—"

"Stop, okay?" He rubbed his temple with his free hand. "Isn't it bad enough I'm accused of a murder I didn't commit, my head is about to explode, and frankly, lady, I want to detach you as much as you want to be detached. So, get the key."

She huffed, tried to fold her arms—one of her favorite gestures—only to realize she couldn't, which infuriated her despite the fact that this annoying situation continued because of her own decisions. Reminding herself of her ploy, she forced herself to breathe calmly.

"What key?" she asked innocently.

His brows crossed. "Don't kid around. I know you cops

all have universal keys for handcuffs. That's why it doesn't matter who puts them on or takes them off. So where do you keep yours?"

She gave him a look that could cut through steel. "I gave my cuffs and key to the officer at the crime scene because he had put his on you. They're what you're wearing."

His eyes narrowed suspiciously, then he reached into his pocket and took out his key ring. On it was a miniature pocketknife set. "All right, Inspector, if that's how you want to play it." From the set, he pulled a toothpick-like steel implement.

"Where did you get that? I thought we emptied your pockets."

He shrugged. "Maybe when the cop leading me to his squad car hit the dirt, he dropped the bag with my keys, cell phone, and wallet. You'll have to ask him."

She shut her eyes a moment, looking for strength. "Before you do anything else, put my Beretta back under the mattress."

He had put the gun under the mattress on "his" side of the bed, retrieved it, and slid it under "hers."

Then the two marched into the other room and sat at the small kitchen table so he could keep the cuffs steady as he began to pick at the lock. Nothing happened. "I don't know why it's not working," he said, closely and cautiously eying her. "I've always opened them this way."

"Maybe it's because the cuffs were changed recently since too many crooks knew how to get the old ones off!" she shouted. She didn't like the way she turned into a raging harridan whenever around Richie Amalfi. Usually, she was completely cool and collected.

He kept trying, then he slammed down the pick. "Hell! My hands are shaking. I need coffee. I can't take your yelling, and I've got to take a leak, too."

The two marched towards the bathroom like condemned men to a gallows. The tiny space off the bedroom held a toilet, basin, shower over the tub, and—since Spike was such a small dog and Rebecca's hours so irregular—Spike's "cat litter" box.

"Me first," Rebecca said, sidling past him. If she sat sideways on the seat, her arm reached the door, which she closed as much as possible against the links of the handcuffs. "Don't look, and don't listen!"

They soon switched sides. While Richie sounded like Niagara Falls, she stood in the bedroom contemplating her next move. Should she remove the handcuffs, or let this farce continue awhile? She decided to see what he would do next.

They shared the sink to wash their hands and faces and comb their hair. She found it completely disgusting that he used her toothbrush. Some things were not made for sharing. She remembered a time when she was younger and 'cooler.' Back then, she always had an extra toothbrush in her apartment, just in case it might be needed. Now, not so much.

Next, he insisted on shaving. Not being partial to blue-black jowls, she gave him the razor she used on her legs. He then demanded a new blade. Some people were so fussy.

As she waited for him to finish, she knew what a Siamese twin felt like, or to be politically correct like all of San Francisco, a conjoined twin. Whatever, it wasn't pleasant.

Back at the kitchen table, he picked at the handcuffs a little longer. "Do you have a file?" he asked.

"A fingernail file?"

"No. A big one. To saw these things in half."

She socked him in the arm. Hard.

oOo

Richie would have liked to pace back and forth across the kitchen as he listened to the messages on his cell phone but he could only manage a few steps each way. Rebecca sat on a chair. She stretched out her arm and when fully extended, he had to cross back the other way. He couldn't help but wonder what kind of game she had decided to play, but he was more than willing to go along. At least she hadn't gone all rulebook on him and turned him in. He knew they were going to have to talk—he only hoped he could be persuasive.

Messages completed, he placed a call. "Shay, it's me. You heard?" he asked. He gave out Rebecca's address. "Come over. Bring Vito." He hung up.

"Shay and Vito?" Her lip curled. "Who are those guys?"

"They work for me."

"Sure. In 'transportation,' right?"

He smirked. "You got it."

"Forget it! In the light of day, and after getting some sleep, I can see that all this is a really bad idea. Come with me to Homicide. Give yourself up and it'll go easier on you. We'll say you gave yourself up to me and then I'll work to get you released so we can figure out who the real killer is."

"Yeah, they'll be all soft and cuddly as they escort me to get the needle! No way, Inspector. I'm not a fan of lethal injections, especially not ones that go into my arm." He spun around and found he could reach a cupboard. He opened the door and perused her supply of dry and canned food. "What've you got that's good to eat around here?"

"If you think I'm going to cook—"

He swung the door shut. "Don't worry. I wouldn't trust you to. But first, there's something I've got to do."

He pulled out a kitchen chair and sat, then picked up the

cell phone and stared at it. He put it down, stood, ran a hand over the back of his head, his face, then sat again and picked up the phone once more. He stared at it, then the ceiling, put the phone down, took a deep breath, tugged his ear lobe, and studied the cell phone once more.

She couldn't take it. *"What the hell are you doing?"*

He didn't answer, didn't even look her way, but hit a button on speed dial, and picked up the phone.

"Hey, Ma, it's—" He swallowed the rest of his words and listened.

"Already?" he said. "I didn't think they'd show up so fast ... I'm sorry, Ma ... I'm okay, really ..." He held the phone away from his ear a moment. Rebecca couldn't hear the words, but the tone of voice reminded her of when she was a little girl and did something her parents called "very disappointing."

"I can't come by. What if they're watching your house?"

She noticed his arm kept twitching as he talked, and at first she didn't understand why. Then she got it. With one hand attached to Rebecca, the other holding the phone, and him being Italian, he was finding it difficult to communicate. Frustrated, he stood and tried to pace again, only to be hauled back by Rebecca. He scowled at her and sat again. "I'm fine, really. Yeah, somebody's taking care of me. Don't worry. Okay. Okay. Five o'clock. I'll try, Ma. Really. Don't cry! And stop worrying. It'll be...I know. I know. Love you, too."

He hung up and glanced at Rebecca. He looked sheepish, then he shrugged. "Mothers," he said, then jumped to his feet. She found herself dragged towards the refrigerator.

"Hey!" she protested, but it quickly died when he handed her a carton of eggs, and on top of it put a cube of butter and a brick of cheddar cheese. "Play nice, Inspector," he said, "and I'll make you a cheese scramble."

She felt tempted to stand pat and make life hard on him. On the other hand, she was starving and needed her wits and her strength to get this nonsense over with as soon as possible. She cooperated.

"Do you have any bread for toast?" he asked.

With only a few yanks, tugs, and curses, she put on toast and coffee while he scrambled eggs and then cooked them with grated cheddar.

He nearly gagged when she poured Tabasco on her eggs, but other than that, they ate in relative peace. They had just finished when they heard a knock on the door.

Richie's eyes went wide then narrowed and he headed towards the shoulder bag with her Glock inside. She stood her ground, tugging on the handcuffs and refusing to let him get close to it.

He frowned, but walked with her to the door. "Get rid of whoever it is," he ordered. As she opened the door just a little way, he stood behind it.

As she had expected, her landlord, Bradley Frick, had knocked. He stood before her with a big smile. Over the years, they had become good friends. He would come down the back stairs to her place, or she'd run up to his, and they often had long heart-to-hearts over coffee or wine, depending on the hour and if Rebecca was on-call or not.

"Rebecca, sweetie, I wanted to be sure you're okay." He wore tight, nearly white jeans, a floral shirt and sandals without socks even though the temperature was chilly. His bleached blond hair spiked around his head, and he had no sideburns while his eyebrows remained dark. His teeth were perfectly capped. "I heard about a murder at a nightclub last night, and since you were on-call, I wondered what happened. The news is so bad in this town! Spike! Come give us a kiss!" He expected her to let him into the house as he bent towards the dog. Instead Rebecca moved her foot so Spike could run to Bradley.

He picked up the dog and cuddled him.

"The case is nearly solved already," she said, feeling awkward about the way she blocked the door. She always invited Bradley in. "There's nothing to worry about, but could you do me a favor and keep Spike with you today? I know I'm going to be working crazy hours, and some people might come by to discuss the case and I don't want him underfoot."

"They're coming *here?*" His eyes opened wide. "You mean like your detective friends and all? To talk about *murder?*"

"Yes. In fact—ouch!"

He jumped nearly ten feet in the air. "What is it?"

"Nothing. Don't worry about it. Good-bye. And thanks, Bradley."

She shut the door and kicked Richie. "That's for trying to break my thumb! What's the matter with you?"

He rubbed his shin. "Whatever it takes, Inspector. You were too chatty all of a sudden."

"Believe me, you're safe from Bradley."

Richie grinned. "That's a relief. I was so, so scared."

"You're not funny, Amalfi!"

Another knock sounded on the door.

"Don't tell me the idiot's come back," Richie said. "Get rid of him this time!"

Glaring at him, she pulled the door open.

And gasped.

One of the most beautiful men she had ever seen in her life stood in the doorway. About six-foot-three, with wavy blond hair, blue eyes and a deep tan, he had high, pronounced cheekbones and as aristocratic a nose as she could imagine. He wore a brown and gray tweed jacket, brown slacks, a white shirt, and a plaid wool neck scarf. "Inspector Mayfield?" he asked politely. Even his voice was magnificent.

She could only gape a moment, then her mouth shut as she wondered how he'd gotten through the locked door to the breezeway ... unless Bradley had let him in. If so, the landlord would be back soon demanding a proper introduction.

"Who—" she began when Richie pulled the door out of her hand and opened it wide.

"Shay, get in here."

That's Shay?

"Where's Vito?" Richie asked.

"Right behind me. He's checking the place out." Shay noticed the handcuffs. Eyes eerily like dry ice traveled over Rebecca from her barely brushed hair to her slept-in outfit. One eyebrow lifted. Who was this guy? she wondered.

Shay glanced back over his shoulder and nodded, then entered the apartment. Following him came the exact type man Rebecca expected to find hanging around Richie Amalfi—a stereotypical wise guy's bodyguard. Vito was sturdy and squat, firmly earthbound, with a cone-shaped head, a fleshy nose, and rolls of fat under his cheeks like melting scoops on an ice cream cone. He wore a a heavy tan car coat with bulging pockets that made Rebecca wonder what he carried in them.

"'Ey, Richie," Vito said, grinning and pointing at the handcuffs. "I heard you was suspected of shooting somebody, not getting hitched."

"Funny. She's a homicide inspector."

He eyed her. "Still, nice *braccioli*." He smirked, then took a bite out of a half-eaten hero sandwich buried in his thick hand. "You here all night, huh? Leave it to you, *paisan*."

"Man, you don't know how scary that thought is." Richie didn't even smile, but just shook his head.

"If you two are talking about what I think you're talking about," Rebecca said, one hand on her hip, "you're both asking for a fat lip." Her eyes shot daggers at Richie. *Just what was so scary?*

Vito's thick brows rose high. Richie hunched his shoulders, then said, "There's coffee. Help yourselves."

"Everybody, *stop!*" Fuming, Rebecca spun towards Richie. "Who are these men? What are their full names?"

"Shay is a nickname," Richie said. "He likes it more than his own name, Henry Tate. And this is Vito Grazioso. Gentlemen, meet Inspector Rebecca Mayfield."

She eyed them. "Are you ex-cons?"

"What you been tellin' her, Richie?" Vito asked.

"They aren't," Richie said. "They walk the straight and narrow. Just like me."

"Sure, you do," she said, then lifted her handcuffed wrist. "You expect me to believe that?"

Instead of answering, Richie said, "Rebecca, sit down at the table."

She studied the men before her. Whoever these men were, whatever was going on, could prove very interesting. Richie surely knew a lot more about the dead woman than he had admitted to. To prove his innocence, he would have to tell Shay and Vito what he knew. She was all ears. This was exactly why she had decided to stick—literally—to Richie. Without a word, she sat, just as Richie asked her to.

Even he looked surprised.

Shay found a cup and saucer rather than a mug for his coffee, as well as a sugar bowl and teaspoon. He sat across from them at the small round table, and meticulously added two and a half spoons of sugar. When he stirred, he decorously extended his little finger. He wore no jewelry, as opposed to Vito who wore a pancake-sized watch and a gold pinky ring so thick and heavy it looked like the Mother Lode.

Rebecca couldn't wrap her head around these three very different men working together.

While Shay sipped coffee and Vito gobbled his sandwich, licked the mayonnaise off his fingers and wiped them on his sweatpants, Richie filled them in on what happened at Big Caesar's.

"*Fung gool,*" Vito swore.

"You're right, but watch your mouth," Richie said, with a quick glance at Rebecca.

"*Fung gool?*" she repeated. "What's that? It doesn't sound Italian."

Richie scowled at her. "Don't say it! It's San Francisco Italian. From Calabrese, Sicilian, who knows? But it's not something you should ever say, all right?"

She blinked in amazement at his reaction.

"Sorry, boss," Vito muttered as he got up, poured coffee into a mug, and then slurped it loudly while returning to the table. "Anyway, you ain't never seen the killer before, right?"

"Never, but he knew his way around, so somebody helped him," Richie replied. "Somebody we know— somebody who set me up, dammit to hell!"

"Who woulda known you was goin' to Big Caesar's last night?" Vito asked.

"Hey, it was Saturday night. Big race at Santa Anita today." Richie twisted in his chair to glance towards Rebecca's TV, and grimaced. Not only wasn't it a plasma, it wasn't even an LCD, but was big and boxy. "They expected me. Besides, the woman I went with—the one who was killed—wanted to go."

"That don't narrow the field none, do it?" Vito said morosely. "But was Danny there?"

Richie shrugged. "Nobody saw him, which was weird. He's always there Saturday night." He faced Rebecca. "Did anyone see him?"

"You're talking about Danny Pasternak, the bookkeeper?" she asked, putting together the talk about horse races and the money man.

"Yeah. Sure."

"No one saw him. And I was told he didn't work nights," Rebecca said. The way the three looked at her, she knew she had been lied to in more ways than one. "So Danny's a bookie?"

Shay and Vito looked at Richie. He nodded. "Well, I guess, yeah, you could say that."

Rebecca threw up the one hand not manacled to Richie. "Great. I'm going to talk to him today. I guess now, my questions will be a bit different than what I had planned as I try to find out why Meaghan Blakely, or whatever her name was, went into his office."

"That wasn't her name?" Richie asked.

"I doubt it. No one with that name came close to fitting her age or description."

"Shit," Richie muttered.

Vito nodded.

Shay said nothing, but looked from one to the other without expression. She had seen eyes that cold only once before, on a known psychopath. What was with him? she wondered, and then, as if he were reading her mind, he gazed at her so intently he seemed like some alien creature intent on turning her into a pod person. The man gave her cold chills. She wondered how she ever found him handsome.

Richie glanced at his watch. "Look at the time." He again eyed her small television. "I don't suppose it's hooked up to a satellite, right, Inspector?"

"Are you joking?"

"DirecTV. Dish. What's to joke about?" His voice became increasingly more desperate as she stared steadily at him. Then his shoulders slumped. "Christ, I don't understand people who don't watch TV properly."

Vito shook his head sympathetically.

Shay abruptly changed the subject. "Why her?" he asked, his thumb pointed towards Rebecca. She realized he must have taken as much of a dislike to her as she had to him.

"She'll have access to stuff we don't," Richie said. "Besides, she knows I didn't kill that woman. She'll work with us."

"Is that so?" Rebecca asked, stunned by the man's arrogance.

"You know I didn't kill anybody," he said.

"I know no such thing." She lifted her handcuffed wrist. "Seems to me you're capable of it."

"You two," Richie said, pointing to Shay and Vito, "find out what you can from Harrison Sidwell and his bouncers. For sure, they know more than they let on to the cops. And I want to know who handed me the note to go see Danny." He turned to Rebecca. "You got the note, right?"

"No one found a note, Amalfi," she said coldly. "And none of the staff admitted to any contact with you other than bringing the drinks you ordered. None of them admitted to seeing Pasternak in the club last night. That part of your story has more holes than Swiss cheese."

Richie shook his head. "If I didn't get the note, I never would have found Meaghan! I wouldn't have been blamed for offing her! Who is she? Why did anyone want her popped? Why hire some hit man to whack her? And where the hell was Danny last night?"

"Wait—*hit* man?" she asked. "Where did that come from?"

"One shot, through the heart. Quiet. Ski mask. Looks like a button with a contract to me." Richie turned towards his friends for confirmation and both nodded as if no sensible person would have thought otherwise.

"Or a very lucky shot," she tossed back at them.

"Right," Richie said, not bothering to hide his contempt ... again.

Richie turned back to his buddies. "Talk to Danny. If he's not home or at work, he could be holed up with his goomar. Carolina Fontana. He set her up in an apartment near North Beach. That's all I know."

"*Goomar?*" Rebecca asked.

"His mistress, what else?" Richie said.

Rebecca had to admit it would probably have taken her a while to find anyone who'd reveal that Danny Pasternak, bookie, had a woman on the side.

"What you gonna do?" Vito asked Richie.

"I gotta get home, get some stuff."

"How you gonna do that?"

Richie looked at Shay who reached into his jacket pocket and handed Richie a burner cell phone and a garage door opener. "They're both set to work," Shay said.

"Good job," Richie said, then turned towards Rebecca. "Ready?"

She all but spat out the words, "Not on your life!"

Chapter 4

RICHIE HELD THE CELL phone to Rebecca's ear as she called Bill Sutter. She hated driving her black Ford Explorer one-handed, especially when she needed to turn a corner. "Sutter, it's me. How's the case coming?"

"We've got the murder weapon, no question about it. It's got Amalfi's fingerprints. We've put out an APB on him. Paavo's fiancée, Angie, is here kicking up a fuss that her cousin's innocent. Another cousin is a lawyer and is here to represent him, if and when he shows up. And everybody's wondering where you are."

"I'm on the case, where else?" she said. "Who's the gun registered to?"

"It isn't."

Why didn't that surprise her?

"When you coming in?" he asked.

"A couple of things came up last night that I want to check out, then I'll be there."

"Really? What things?"

"I ... uh, it's complicated. Listen, did you reach Danny Pasternak yet?"

"Can't find him. His old lady said he didn't come home last night, but she isn't worried. Seems he spends a lot of nights away. She claims she doesn't know where. Sounds like he's got something on the side, if you know what I mean."

"Okay, thanks. Talk to you later." She nodded for Richie to hit the "End" button. He did.

"You've got a lawyer," she said and told him briefly about the conversation.

He directed her to a narrow street near the top of Twin Peaks, an expensive neighborhood of mid-century modern and newer homes with garages on the ground floor and living areas above. "It's number eighty-one on the left. Gray. Big picture window," Richie said as he tried to hide in the leg area under the glove compartment. She covered him with a blanket and plopped her handbag on top of it.

She knew she was breaking more rules than a leopard had spots, but for some reason, she—who was normally such a by-the-book person in everything—was unable to stop herself. She had thought long and hard about getting Richie into her SUV, and then removing the handcuff from her own wrist, putting it on his, and arresting him. She was armed, of course, and it would have been easy. He knew it, too. But he trusted her.

That was his problem not hers, she told herself. She had a job to do. Right now, she simply wanted to learn why he decided to go to his house and what he expected to find there. And then she would arrest him. She needed to play along just a little while longer.

She spotted the house he described up ahead.

An unmarked police car sat two doors before it. She stopped in the middle of the block, rolled down her window, and stuck her head and one free arm out.

"Mayfield, Homicide," she called, showing her badge. "You guys can take a half-hour break. I'm going to check around inside. It'll take me a while."

"You sure you don't want back-up?" one of the patrolmen asked.

"What did you say?" She let her voice grow loud and hostile. "You think I can't handle myself? Is that it? Why? Because I'm female, maybe? You think I'm not capable of doing my job? Let me remind you, *officer*, I'm in Homicide."

"No, ma'am. I mean, yes, ma'am." The guy didn't say another word, just gave a nod to his partner and the two sped off as Rebecca pulled into Richie's driveway.

"Good thinking," Richie said, popping his head out from under the blanket. "But for a minute I thought you were going to give the kid a spanking."

She threw the blanket back over his head.

He fought his way free, took the garage door opener out of his pocket and hit one of the buttons. The two-car garage door opened. A 700-series BMW sedan was parked on one side. She should have known Richie would own more than one car...unless he lived with someone. A girlfriend maybe?

But he had dated Meaghan Blakely.

Two-timing rat!

"Who does that car belong to?" she asked.

"It's mine. Sometimes a Porsche is too small. " He glanced at her. "Why?"

Rebecca ignored his question and drove into the garage. "I hope you realize that if those cops are watching, they're going to wonder where I got your garage opener."

"Better they wonder that than see me waltz you up to my front door and open it with a key."

She knew he was right, but for some reason that only increased her irritation. He hit the remote again and the garage door lowered shut behind them. "Come this way," she said, opening the door on the driver's side.

He stubbornly shook his head, then put his hands

together and cracked his knuckles. At each pop, a ripple went down her back. God but he was annoying! "I already crawled over the car seats when we got into this piece of junk," he said. "Now, it's your turn."

"You can't believe how much I hate you." She stepped out of the driver's door and tugged on the handcuffs. "At least my car doesn't have bucket seats with a gear shift and handbrake in the center. Be thankful and come on."

He sat like an immovable object. "That's only because they didn't make bucket seats in nineteen-fifty! But you've still got this arm rest between the seats. So it's your turn."

She did a slow burn, yet the inside of his house might turn up some evidence that would prove his guilt or innocence, and entering with him would make it easy to search. "Fine. Go!" She crawled over the seats and out the passenger door.

He unlocked the door between the garage and the house, and they walked up a flight of stairs.

The sunny kitchen was bright with white cabinets and pale blue, gray, and white granite countertops. But the cabinet doors and drawers all hung open, and the room smelled of gas.

"What the...!" Richie ran across the room, Rebecca doing her best to help, as he flung open the window over the sink, then hurried to the gas cooktop and shut off the burners. They were unlit and caused gas to fill the house.

A whirring sound continued. The two stood absolutely still, then both turned towards the microwave. It was running.

"Get out of here!" Rebecca cried, tugging on Richie's arm to leave the kitchen. She could have been trying to pull a brick wall.

Her feet were nearly lifted out of her boots as he lunged

45

towards the microwave and punched the button to open the door. Inside she saw a bowl with rice in it. It had started to blacken. The rice was a built-in timing device. Set the microwave to run for an hour or more, put the rice inside, and wait for it to dry out enough to catch fire. When it did, with the gas leak, the whole house would have gone up.

A shudder went through Richie that Rebecca could feel through the handcuffs.

Although most of his swear words were in Italian— including the infamous *'fung gool'*—she didn't need a translation.

Five minutes later, they would have been too late to save the house. Four minutes later, they would have been cinders.

"Let's get all the windows open," she said, feeling a little squeamish. They stepped into the living room. The big picture window gave a breathtaking view of San Francisco, looking eastward, towards the downtown and financial district skyscrapers. But Rebecca scarcely noticed as she and Richie went to the smaller side windows and opened them wide.

That done, she watched Richie's expression move from shock to sadness as he eyed the destruction to his home.

The furniture had been slashed, and its stuffing pulled out. The huge, wide-screen plasma television set lay smashed on the floor, its back pried off and tossed aside.

"My God," she murmured. "How could they have done this with the police watching the house? Unless"—she faced him—"they did it before you escaped from Bill Sutter. Before you became a suspect."

He didn't answer but walked down the hall. There was a small guest bedroom, a den, and a large master bedroom. They had all been ransacked the way the living room had been. In the bedroom, three TV sets had been aligned on stands facing the bed—a king. Now, all had been destroyed as if someone searched inside them. But for what? she wondered. Exactly what was Richie not telling her?

Richie no longer seemed sad, and no longer swore. He no longer said anything, but in a fierce, all-consuming fury marched through the house, alternately kicking some broken pieces and sadly glowering at others as he absorbed the destruction.

She wasn't sure if his silence or his cursing was worse.

He stopped suddenly and picked up a small, framed black-and-white picture of a young man. He was thin, wearing jeans, a plaid shirt with the sleeves rolled up to his elbows, smoking a cigarette and leaning against an old Plymouth sedan. He was good-looking, with fairly long, thick black hair and heavy-lidded dark eyes much like Richie's. The whole photo had the look of something out of the sixties or seventies.

The glass covering the photo had been smashed. "Why'd they do this?" Richie muttered. She knew he expected no answer from her.

"Who was he?" Rebecca asked.

"My father. It's my favorite picture of him, taken when he was young, hopeful, and maybe a little reckless, before everything went to hell for him. He died when I was only five, but I kind of remember him. Or, at least, I tell myself I do." He stood the photo with the broken glass up on a shelf, and Rebecca could sense his sorrow as he did so.

Richie opened more windows throughout the house and then led her out the back door off the kitchen to clear their heads and wait for the smell of gas to dissipate.

"Want to sit?" Richie asked, pointing at the stairs. It was warm outdoors, which was a good thing since they had discovered earlier as they left her apartment that being stuck together with handcuffs made it impossible for them to put their jackets on.

"Sure."

They sat side-by-side, facing his garden. Richie's feet were wide spread, his free arm flung casually across one thigh. She sat with her knees together, her free arm wrapped around them. Their cuffed hands were between them, palms resting on the step they sat on.

She tried to imagine what was going through his head after all that had happened since last night. More than anything, he looked deflated, and every bit his age, which Paavo once told her was around thirty-nine or forty. Crow's feet lined the outer corners of his eyes, and curved lines—laugh lines they were usually called but not, she thought, in his case—creased the edges of his mouth. His face was fairly thin, and his nose high and long—a very Italian face, to her Nordic eye.

In the sunlight, his hair was so black it had no trace of brown, and only the temples held a few gray strands. His eyes often appeared as black as his hair, yet in the sunlight she could see flecks of brown and even green in them.

He wasn't buff, but not soft and flabby either. He no longer had the lithe, slim body of a young man, but had the solid build of someone mature and strong. And while he wasn't movie-star handsome, something about him, especially around the eyes, and the nose, and the mouth, and definitely the somewhat long, rakish way he wore his hair, reminded her of Al Pacino back when she was young and he was a heartthrob, until she learned he was only about five feet seven inches tall, which meant he would barely reach her nose. At least Richie was taller than that. In all, there was nothing she disliked about his looks. Not that it mattered one way or the other.

She swallowed hard and forced her gaze down to the handcuffs, trying to rekindle her anger and suspicion.

Beside his, her hand was white and pale, the color of someone who did most of her work indoors or at night. His skin was olive and deeply tanned, and half-again as broad as hers. It made her wonder once more how he spent his days.

She averted her eyes from him altogether. Any good detective had a duty to notice details about people, places, and things. That was all she was doing.

She turned her attention to the simple but well-tended yard. The sun felt good on her face, and the smell of the lawn, flowers and shrubs a reminder that life offered more than dead bodies and finding murderers. In a corner she noticed a small vegetable garden. "Did you plant that?"

"Sure. You can't buy tomatoes that taste good anymore. Same with peppers and zucchini. Even artichokes. They grow easily here, except the artichoke, but I'm working on it. I like to grow my own herbs as well. Over there, to the right, you'll see basil, oregano, garlic, onions, and fennel."

"It's nice," she said, then added, "We used to have a farm in Idaho. My father grew potatoes and corn. That's how he supported us. At harvest time, everyone in the family helped. We also had a vegetable garden."

He faced her. "You were a farm girl?"

She gave a small smile. "I left because it was too much work. I wanted something easier, like being a cop in San Francisco."

He smiled at her attempt at a joke. "Do your parents still farm?"

"No. My dad passed away when I was twenty-three, and my mom sold the business to my uncle, my father's brother. She lives in Boise, my sister in Los Angeles, and I'm here."

"Do you ever miss it?" he asked.

She thought a moment. "I loved it as a kid, loved the way my dad would strut around, so proud of how tall his corn grew." She smiled at a memory. "My sister and I would sometimes hide in the cornfield and then jump out when we thought our parents couldn't find us. Thinking back now, I'm pretty sure they knew exactly where we hid, and went along with our game."

"Don't get me started on ways to torment a parent." Richie said with a laugh.

She liked his laugh, liked the way expression filled his whole face, especially his eyes, as he spoke, and laughed, and smiled. She found it hard to look away from him. "I guess you did a bit more than hide," she said.

"My mom would have been on her knees thanking God if that was all," he said, then his face fell, and she imagined his thoughts turned to the police contacting his mother last night, and to his father's picture on the floor, the glass cracked.

Despite herself, she sympathized with what had happened to him, and his loss. "Your home looked like it was lovely."

"Yeah. It *was*. You got that right."

"At least it wasn't destroyed. Furniture is easily replaced."

"Thank God." He reached over to the box hedge beside him and rubbed a leaf. "I surprised my friends and relatives when I bought this place, it being outside of the old neighborhood and all. But sometimes a guy likes to have a little peace and quiet, you know. Nobody living upstairs or down, a little garden. I thought I'd found a refuge. No more, though."

"You'll fix it up. It'll be fine," she said.

"Maybe." Brooding, he stared out at the lawn. "I'm going

to find whoever's behind this, Rebecca. They'll be sorry they decided to mess with me."

"What were you hiding in the house?" she asked. At his sudden harsh stare, she added, "Don't tell me nothing. It's time to come clean about everything that's going on. It's the only way I can help you."

"Damn!" he murmured, then louder. "You're way off base."

"I told you, don't say that!"

"What do you want me to say?" He scarcely moved, and his voice had turned so cold, so hard, it hit deep in her gut. All in all, she preferred her fidgeting, emotional Richie to this icy one.."Do you think I want somebody to blow up my home? It's bad enough they trashed the place. I don't know what they're looking for. I don't have anything ... much."

"You're lying to me!" she insisted.

"I'm hiding nothing! Okay? Nothing." He all but snarled at her, then turned away with a shake of his head. "You're so damn suspicious!" He went back to brooding.

"You came back here for a reason. What was it?"

He rubbed his forehead. "That's not important anymore. It's all changed."

Just then, his phone rang.

He mostly listened, only saying a word or two. When he hung up, he stood and faced Rebecca. "Nobody seems to know where Danny Pasternak is."

She stared up at him, not moving. "How do you know that?"

"Vito tried to find him, and couldn't. I'm not surprised the cops couldn't find him, but Vito should have been able to. Something's wrong, Rebecca. I wonder if something happened to Danny."

She stood facing him, the handcuffs keeping them much

too close together. "We'll have to find out."

"Shay found a place on Telegraph Hill that might have some answers," he said. "Let's get out of here."

"One minute while I call the Crime Scene techs," she said. "I want them to dust your house for prints or any indication of who might have broken in here."

"No."

"No?"

"The guys who do this sort of thing are pros. They don't leave prints. All you'll get are a bunch of prints from people who the law might have some interest in for a variety of reasons, but don't want to harm me. I won't allow it."

She wanted to argue with him, but even more important was to find out those "answers" he referred to on Telegraph Hill.

"What if I just take the bowl that had the rice in it," she said. "Testing it will tell us a lot, or nothing."

He nodded. "You're wasting your time, but I don't care. Fine, do it."

They returned to the kitchen. She placed the bowl in a zip-lock bag, then they left the house.

Never in her life had she associated with anyone who seemed so much like he should be guilty, yet still caused her to believe in his innocence.

She wasn't sure why she believed him, but she would stake her life on it. And considering that she had let him drag her into a house that could have been blown to kingdom come, she already had.

Chapter 5

RICHIE GRIPPED REBECCA'S hand and then draped a dark blue pullover sweater he had picked up at his house in a way that covered their joined hands and handcuffs. "That works," he said.

"That looks dumb. Nobody carries a sweater that way," she protested.

"Yeah, it's weird, but it's better than letting anyone see the cuffs. It looks less strange if we stand close together."

"Terrific." The word was a sneer.

He kept her close as they walked up to the doorman of a high-rise apartment on the east side of Telegraph Hill near the waterfront. Richie's friends had found Danny's *goomar's* apartment, and they were there to talk to her.

"We're here to see Miss Fontana," Richie said. "Vito Grazioso and friend."

"I'll let her know some guests have arrived." The doorman picked up the phone and spoke softly, then faced them. "Twentieth floor, apartment twenty-o-one."

Richie paled. His mouth opened then closed, and finally he whisked her over to a corner and said quietly, "Let's forget it."

Why? she wondered. Then she smirked. "You're afraid of

heights."

His gaze shifted from the doorman, to the elevator, to her. "Of course I'm not! But what's wrong with Danny's woman? She think she's an eagle up there?" He stuck his hand in his pocket and pouted. "Hell, I might get a nose bleed."

She couldn't help but smile. If she hadn't seen it, she wouldn't have believed it. "I'll hold your nostrils shut if that happens," she said. On occasion, this morning, she would have been tempted to hold his mouth shut at the same time, but not now. Actually, the supposed tough guy's fear of heights was kind of cute. As soon as she thought that, she shuddered, and told herself to forget it. "Cute" was the last thing she wanted to think about Richie!

She steered him towards the elevator where he waited, nervously rocking from heel to toe and jiggling the coins in his pocket. Rebecca moved closer to him to better hide the handcuffs from the doorman. If he spotted them, he'd most likely call 911. Then she would have to arrest Richie. And more than ever, she didn't want to.

The elevator doors opened and she shoved Richie on ahead of her so he wouldn't bolt and let the handcuffs be seen. As it began to move, his hand under the sweater tightened on hers. The higher they rose, the harder he squeezed until she feared she'd have crushed knuckles before the fifteenth floor, let alone the twentieth.

When it stopped, he leaped off faster than if fired from a slingshot. She tumbled out against him, her arm going around him, clutching him, to stop from falling. She quickly jumped back, but he seemed too busy deep breathing to even notice.

He quickly found 2001 and knocked on the door. A blond woman opened it and then stared at them with seriously curled eyelashes covered with gobs of mascara and eyebrows waxed and penciled into high, thin arches. The combination made her appear perpetually astonished.

"Richie? Where's Vito?" She stepped out of the apartment and glanced towards the elevator after giving Rebecca a quick once-over. Her features were pinched, her eyes small despite her tricks to make them seem larger, and even her teeth looked tiny and thin.

"I didn't feel like giving the doorman my name."

"That's okay, Richie. You know how much I like seeing you." Richie followed her into the apartment, half-dragging Rebecca with him.

Carolina Fontana wore a tight scoop-necked black knit top that showed off enormous round balls of silicone where her breasts ought to be, skin-tight black Capri pants that left nothing to the imagination, and sky-high black stiletto sandals. "Vito told me you might come by to see me, Richie. I tried to fix my face for you," she said in a breathless voice as she wrapped her arms around his neck. "Thanks for coming. I'm worried about Danny! I'll do whatever I can to help you."

"I know, sweetheart," he said, holding her close with his one free arm. Her waist was tiny, and her behind so round and protruding Rebecca wondered if a little surgery hadn't been performed there as well. She stood beside them— unseen, unnoticed, and obviously unwelcomed.

Carolina took a half-step back, clutching the front of Richie's shirt. "I heard what they been saying about you, Richie," she emoted, "but I didn't believe it. Not for a minute. Not Richie, I said to myself. That Richie, he's one of the good guys."

"Thanks, Carolina. I was hoping you knew I'd never hurt a hair on a woman's head. Is Danny here?"

She broke into sobs on his shoulder. "I don't know

where he is. You got to believe me."

"Look, was something going on between Danny and the dead woman? I mean, I know he was always faithful to you. He loved you. But he had to have known her since she was killed in his office, right?"

Rebecca couldn't take much more of this. She could feel her gorge rising. "Her name was Meaghan Blakely, by the way."

Carolina didn't bother to look at her. "I have no idea who she was, or what she meant to my Danny." Her sobs, snuffles, and catches in the throat grew louder.

Rebecca turned away from Carolina's theatrics. Looking over the apartment with its beautiful bay view, French provincial furnishings, and tasteful artwork, she couldn't help but suspect that Ms. Fontana's tears were more over worry about what all this might mean for Danny's future—and ultimately her own. If Danny was involved in this murder, Carolina would need to find someone else to pick up the bill for her, and from the way she held on to Richie as he continued his one handed comforting—and Rebecca couldn't help but wonder just how thorough his comforting would be if she weren't attached to his other hand—it appeared Carolina considered him a prime candidate.

But then she noticed that Richie was looking at her. She met his gaze and he rolled his eyes, as if to say he knew exactly what Carolina was up to.

Rebecca grinned slightly, then nodded. She coughed, then coughed again.

Carolina peeled herself off Richie like skin from a banana, starting at the head and only slowly easing her body away from his one centimeter at a time. "Oh, excuse me," she said, eying Rebecca. Despite her sobs, her eyes were dry. No running mascara for her. "How rude of me." She stuck out her hand. "Carolina Fontana."

Despite the Italian-sounding surname, her first name was pronounced like the southern states: Car-o-*lye*-na, as in 'nothing could be finah.' Since Richie held Rebecca's right hand, she had to grasp Carolina's with her left and gave a weak squeeze that she hoped appeared to be comforting. "I'm—"

"Becky Jones," Richie said quickly. "A friend."

Carolina's eyes zeroed in like a radar gun on their clasped hands with the sweater over them. "Please sit down." Carolina gestured towards the sofa. She stood with her back ramrod straight, shoulders back, chest out.

Rebecca usually prided herself on having a good, all natural figure. Her proportions were more than adequate and her four-times a week gym workouts had left her well-toned, firm, and shapely in a—not to be too smug about it—attractive way. Still, around Carolina Fontana she felt like a flat-chested teenager. Especially since she still wore last night's jeans and heavy turtleneck. She wondered if Carolina wondered why Richie wore dress slacks but no jacket, and a wrinkled white shirt.

"Would you two like a drink?" Carolina asked.

"Yes," Richie replied.

"No," Rebecca answered at the same time.

Carolina looked confused. "Would you like beer, Richie? Or maybe a high ball?" Then, to Rebecca, "I've got Diet Coke and 7-Up, too."

Richie asked for a beer, Rebecca a Coke as Richie headed for a chair, Rebecca the sofa.

He realized his mistake and stepped to the sofa beside her. They stood, side-by-side, facing it.

Glaring at each other, Rebecca stepped backward, Richie forward, and they made a half-circle. Both ended up with their backs to the sofa, and then they sat.

Carolina watched with mouth agape. "Jeez, you two are sure a couple of lovebirds. Don't want to let go even for a minute."

"Yeah, that's us," Richie said with a devilish smirk as he pressed his shoulder against Rebecca's, his face close to hers, and his voice a low rumble. "Lovebirds."

"Turkey!" Rebecca whispered to him as Carolina went to the bar across the room.

"Mud hen!"

"Capon!"

There was that smirk again, and one eyebrow lifted. "Don't count on it."

She abruptly shut her mouth as Carolina approached with their drinks, still in bottles and cans. She put a can opener on the table. Rebecca and Richie's eyes met. Who knew it took two hands to open a beer bottle or soda can? Rebecca held the containers while Richie opened them. Carolina observed them in wide-eyed amazement.

An open can of Diet Pepsi was on a lamp table and she sat in the chair beside it.

"So Richie, you wanted to see me about something?" Carolina murmured as she kept perusing Rebecca from head to toe and back again with a bewildered what-can-he-possibly-see-in-her question in her eyes.

Rebecca would have loved to wipe that smugly stupid look off Carolina's face, but she kept her mouth shut, knowing that was the best way to learn something, which was, after all, why she was here.

Richie gulped down some beer, then nodded. "All I can figure is Danny must be involved in this thing—whatever it is. I'm hoping he might have said something to you. Was he having trouble with anyone? You women have a sixth sense about your men, especially if he was seeing another woman. Did you get any feeling like that about Danny?"

"God, Richie, I wish I could help you, but everybody loved Danny."

He sipped more beer and let a moment pass. "I know you'd like to think that, but the truth is, Danny was a bookie. He took money from people and placed bets. That meant that if they lost, they had to pay up. Sometimes people don't like to shell out when the money's due, you know?"

"You're right." She walked to the bar and poured a whole lot of bourbon directly into her Pepsi can, not spilling a drop, as if she had done it often. "I don't like to think of that stuff, but you're right."

"Somebody trashed my house," Richie said. "They tried to blow it up. Someone shot my date in Danny's office. Now, nobody seems to know where Danny is, and I'm supposed to take the fall for the dead woman's murder. All that happening within a few hours has to mean it's all connected. What if Danny is involved? What if he's in trouble? In danger? Look, if some guys are after him and I don't stop them, they might come here. They might be after you next."

Carolina's eyes rounded like saucers. "Oh, God! You think so, Richie?"

He nodded.

She swirled the can, brows crossed as if from the strain of thinking. "Danny acted worried, but I'm having trouble remembering why. It was, you know, like not all that interesting to me." She twisted a lock of hair around her finger. "He said, 'Boy, this'll fry 'em.' Then he'd laugh."

"What would fry who?" Richie asked.

She took a few swigs, then brightened. "Maybe you can call me sometime, and I might remember."

"Listen," Richie said, "I don't have time for games."

"Aw, Richie!"

He spoke the next words slowly. "Carolina, tell me right now. I won't ask again." A chill went down Rebecca's back at his harsh and threatening tone. She had never seen that side of him before.

Carolina paled and studied him to see if he was joking. He wasn't. "Hey, now I remember!" she cried, then hurried across the room to sit on the sofa beside Richie, thigh to thigh, her hand on his knee. The sofa had become pretty crowded. "He worried about his book." She smiled, thrilled she could be of help.

"Book?" Richie said. "You mean like his records? His bookie info?"

"No, not that kinda book. A real book. He was writing a book about his life, and gambling, and all the big shots he knew—that kinda tell-all stuff. He even thought about putting in a epi—, uh, epilode? Epilodge? Epi—"

"Epilogue?" Rebecca ventured.

"Yeah, one a those, to give pointers about how to beat the odds. Then, he was gonna retire off of all the money he'd make on the book. And even royalties. And maybe a movie deal. He figured it'd be a best seller for a long time, and him and me could live someplace nice like Aruba. I didn't believe that last part, but he was nice to say it, doncha think?"

"Nice." Richie pondered her words. He glanced at Rebecca. She could tell from his expression how potentially dangerous it could be to write a book about his life as a bookie, especially if he planned to name those so-called "big shots." Danny couldn't be that stupid. Carolina had to be wrong. "Wait a minute," Richie said. "Danny was a great guy, but he was no writer. I mean, he'd send a text message and it'd be damn dull. He was a numbers guy, not a wordsmith."

"Yeah, that's what worried him. But he found somebody

to work with. He called him something like, uh, his ghost. Yeah, that's right. His ghost. Jeez, Richie, do you think that was, like, prophetic?"

Chapter 6

WHAT'S GOING ON, Mayfield?" Bill Sutter demanded hotly. Rebecca had shut off her cell phone ringer when she went into Carolina Fontana's apartment, but while there she had felt it vibrate every five minutes. Once outside, she found a flurry of missed calls from her partner.

"I'm sorry, Bill," she said as she and Richie walked along the sidewalk towards her SUV.

"I need you here! We're the weekend on-call team!"

"Any new cases?"

"Not yet, but at any minute—"

"I know! I'm sick, but I'll be there as soon as I can."

"Sick? Then why the hell didn't you answer the door when I sent Mike Hennessy over to check on you?" Sutter yelled into the phone. She had never heard him that angry before, but then, she had never before done anything to make him angry at her. She held the phone away from her ear as Sutter continued. Richie moved closer so he could listen in.

"Are you going to tell me where you are?" Sutter continued. "Or do I have to send out a posse to find you? It was interesting, by the way, that Hennessy didn't need to be told your address. But that aside, he reported that when you didn't answer, he knocked on your landlord's door. The landlord told him you had some visitors and probably went out with them. What the hell's that supposed to mean? What visitors? Where's 'out'? I want you here, Mayfield!"

"I went to the doctor's," she said calmly. "I shut off the phone so he could listen to my heart and lungs without ring tones messing up my physical."

Richie tried not to laugh.

"Forget it, Mayfield! Your landlord said you didn't look or act sick. You've never been to a doctor in all the time I've known you—and you've come to work in such bad shape the chief had to order you to go home. What are you up to?"

"Look, I'll be there as soon as I can, all right?"

There was a long pause. "Something's not right," Sutter said. "This isn't like you *at all!* For all I know, you're in danger! You check in to Homicide or the nearest station within the hour. That's an order from your senior partner."

"I don't know if it'll be possible."

"That's what worries me. One hour!"

She hung up and then faced Richie. "You heard?"

He nodded. "One more place we need to go, then you can go calm Sutter down."

Whatever could he mean by that? she wondered. "Okay."

He waited as she unlocked the SUV, and then slid over from the driver's side to the passenger seat.

She got in. Awkwardly, they fastened their seat belts. "So," she said, "now that you've spoken to Carolina Fontana, what do you think has happened to Danny Pasternak?"

He turned to her, head cocked, those heavy-lidded eyes studying her. "Right now, I'm more interested in what Bill Sutter said. Why does Officer Hennessy know where you live?"

oOo

Rebecca pulled into a gas station then headed straight for the women's room, Richie in tow. Fortunately, it was empty. He might have the bladder of a bull, but she didn't. When the two of them came out, a woman stood waiting to use the room. She gawked at Richie then Rebecca. "I should tell the manager!" she said.

"Don't bother, lady, he's my prisoner." Rebecca held up her cuffed wrist.

"Prisoner of love." Richie waggled his brows and pointed at Rebecca. "She's very kinky."

The woman gasped, unsure which to believe, eyed the bathroom warily, then turned around and hurried back to her car.

After another brief skirmish at Rebecca's SUV, she and the offensive one came to an understanding: Richie would crawl over the seats to get in, and she would crawl over them to get out. Then they drove away.

Richie phoned Shay and sent him over to Carolina's apartment to see if Danny left any paperwork or computer information there.

"Why didn't you do it while you were there?" Rebecca asked once he hung up the phone.

"Because Shay is better at stuff like that, and I always use the best. Go straight, then left onto Columbus Avenue."

"But why would Carolina allow Shay to go through Danny's things?"

He tugged at his ear. "He can be persuasive."

"He'll threaten her?"

"Of course not." He shrugged. "But he's got his ways."

She didn't like the sound of that.

Richie sat fiddling with the radio, looking in the almost empty glove box, adjusting the outside mirror on the passenger side even though she was the one driving and had found it perfect. Did the guy never stop touching things? He was truly getting on her nerves. Or, it might be more that the longer this crazy situation with him went on, the more frayed her nerves were becoming. If she got caught, she was in for a world of hurt with her job. Or, her *former* job was more like it.

"What does Shay do?" she asked, trying to think of anything besides how much trouble she could be in.

Suddenly every muscle-twitching, ear-tugging, knuckle-cracking, hair-raking movement of his stopped and he stared at her. "Why the interest?" he asked. "Although, I hear a lot of women are attracted to his looks. At first, anyway."

"And then?" Rebecca asked, curious.

His gaze turned enigmatic. "Then, they get to know him."

Richie directed Rebecca into a street lined with two and three-story flats near the very top of Russian Hill. One of them had an open garage door and Richie directed her inside.

"Let's go," Richie said, picking up the sweater they had used to hide the handcuffs from Carolina.

Rebecca refused to move. "Not unless you tell me where we're going."

"I think it's better if you're surprised."

She counted to ten. "No, it isn't."

He took one look at her expression and said, "Okay. We're going to see my mother. Her name's Carmela."

"*What?* You want to pay a visit now?" She climbed over the seats to get out of the car

"I don't want to. I promised. She's worried about me." He led her out the back of the garage to a little yard filled with dead shrubs. An unlocked gate led from that yard to the one butted against it. From there, they went into the garage of the building it belonged to. An interior door opened to a large foyer with a maroon-colored carpet and wooden banisters that led upstairs to two flats. Rebecca felt he was leading her through a maze.

Finally, Richie took her hand and once again draped the sweater he carried over their joined hands and handcuffs to hide them from view. He smoothed his hair, his shirt, straightened his collar, and then knocked on the door of the top flat.

Almost immediately the door flew open. A small, older woman with short, dyed, copper-colored hair and a hawk-like nose stood glaring at Richie. "Richie, what's the matter with you getting mixed up with such people! Are you all right?" Carmela Amalfi put her hands on his shoulders as she studied him head to toe at the same time as she scrutinized Rebecca and, in typical Italian mother fashion, clearly found her wanting.

"Like I said, it's not my fault, and I'm okay." He leaned over and kissed her cheek.

She pushed him away and faced Rebecca.

"Who's this?"

"This is my friend, Reba."

Rebecca took a half-step forward. "Hello, Mrs. Amalfi."

Carmela gave her a curt nod, her eyes narrow. "You're so blond. Your people must come from northern Italy. Milanese, maybe?"

Rebecca glanced at Richie with a *Now what?* look.

He swallowed hard. "She's not Italian, Ma."

"Oh? You didn't tell me her last name. What am I, a mind reader? You said you were looking for a nice Italian girl, so I thought ... seeing as how you two can't seem to let go of each other and all." She grimaced, but also appeared befuddled as her gaze locked on the sweater covering their hands.

"I know, I know." He kissed her cheek again then put his arm around her waist as all three of them walked into the flat. They stood in a hallway with the living room and dining room at one end, the bedrooms at the other, and the kitchen and bathroom in the middle. He backed away from Carmela. "I've got to get something in my bedroom, Ma."

"In your bedroom? Then Reba can stay here with me." She pressed her lips together so fiercely they made her face wrinkle. "As is only proper. *Right?*"

Rebecca gaped, speechless.

"No, I need her with me." Richie headed down the hall, pulling Rebecca behind him. Carmela looked ready to spit.

He whisked Rebecca into a bedroom and quickly shut the door. She found herself in a young boy's paradise, with autographed baseballs, Little League trophies, an army of Transformers, Rock 'Em Sock 'Em Robots, toy trucks and cars, and an arsenal of toy guns and rifles. Even a cowboy holster and hat. "You still have a bedroom in your mother's house?" she asked, stunned.

He was going through the top dresser drawer, which was filled with underwear and socks. "Here it is!"

He held up a handcuff key.

"What every young boy should have," Rebecca said wryly.

"I knew it'd come in handy one of these days." He unlocked the cuff from his own wrist first.

"What is this room, some kind of shrine?" Rebecca held out her wrist so he could remove her cuff as well.

"She says when I have kids they can come and visit. Anyway, she doesn't need this room." He put the handcuffs and the key back inside the dresser drawer and shut it.

"I suggest you don't leave those there, not if your mother's the snooping type. You don't want her to get the wrong idea about you...or, God forbid, me."

"My mother would *never* think of what you're suggesting. You don't talk that way about her. You don't even *think* that way about her. She doesn't know about that sort of stuff."

Sure she doesn't.

Rebecca did her best not to smile as he opened the drawer, removed the scandalous handcuffs and key, and stuffed them into the pocket of his slacks.

"Are you an only child?" she asked, picking up a Transformer action figure and looking it over. She also played with those as a kid.

"Yeah. It was just me and my mom growing up."

"I see," Rebecca murmured, putting down the toy.

"It's not bad being the apple of your mother's eye with no competition. Speaking of which, she's going to break down the door if we don't get out of here."

Rebecca struggled to keep a straight face when Richie opened the door and found Mama Amalfi standing before it, arms crossed, looking ready to burst with indignation and umbrage. He hurried past her, giving her a quick peck on the cheek as he zipped by, then flung his arm around Rebecca's waist and hustled her down the stairs at a fast clip. "Thanks, Ma. Gotta go. I'll call you."

"What do you mean, you're going?" Carmela leaned over the banister and shouted, "I made *pasta fazool* and *gagootz* for you! The way you like them!"

"Freeze them, Ma. I'll be back!"

Only after he got Rebecca out of his mother's garage and into the yard did he stop, let her go, and take a deep breath. She laughed. "And I thought I had it bad with *my* mother," she said.

He looked more frazzled by his mother than he had when he was being arrested. "You mean you get the old 'Why aren't you married yet?' treatment, too?" he asked. "And your mother isn't even Italian or Jewish, right?"

"My mother's family was Swedish, but that hasn't stopped her. She thinks if I were married, I'd give up my job to stay home to be a wife and mother."

He paused, his hand on the door to the garage where her SUV was parked. "Would you?"

"Hell, no! I love what I'm doing. It's interesting and when I get a killer off the streets, immensely satisfying."

"I'm with your mother. I honestly don't see why an Idaho girl would want to be a cop in San Francisco."

She shrugged. "Maybe it was because I loved watching reruns of *The Streets of San Francisco* and hoped to meet a young Michael Douglas. Who knows? Boise's a nice quiet city, a good place to raise a family, but I was young and single and wanted to experience life in a big city."

"How did you end up with the police?"

She rubbed the wrist that had the handcuff on it. "Dumb luck, I had a friend who moved to San Francisco and she made some phone calls for me. The police department had a big push to hire more women. I've always been physically fit, so I took the test. I thought I'd keep the job just long enough to bring in money while I looked around for work I really wanted to do. I never dreamed I'd like it."

"You sound like an adrenaline junkie," he said.

She glanced his way. "Aren't all cops? What's the old saying? Each work day is seven-hours fifty-five minutes of boredom and five minutes of sheer terror. God love it!"

He shook his head. "You can't deny the danger," he said. "Especially in a city like San Francisco. I don't know if I'd want to watch my wife strap on a gun to go off to work every day."

"Hell, that's not only a problem for husbands," she said wryly. "Just dating, I've met plenty of good men who can't handle it. That's why I only go out with cops now. I wouldn't even consider dating a civilian."

"No?" he asked, catching her eye.

"Never." Her tone left no wiggle room.

"I guess that explains Mike Hennessy," he said.

She put her hands on her hips. "Are you a detective now?"

"Is it serious between you two?"

"Good God, no!" He obviously didn't know Mike Hennessy—a nice guy, but watching paint dry was more exciting.

"Are you seeing anyone?" he asked.

"That's rather personal," she said.

"You're right." He nodded. "None of my business."

With that, he opened the door to the garage and let her walk in front of him, heading towards her SUV.

As she unlocked the door and started to get in, Richie bolted for the street.

"Hey!" she yelled, stunned, then took off after him.

A Maserati was waiting, its passenger door open. Richie jumped in and the driver—she was sure it was Shay—took off, nearly going airborne as the car catapulted down the hilly streets.

She turned, ran into the garage, and backed out her SUV, but by the time she tore down the hill and reached the corner, the Maserati was nowhere to be seen.

As she pounded the steering wheel in furious frustration, she muttered words she was sure would make Richie's mother gasp.

Chapter 7

"CATCHING UP ON YOUR beauty sleep, Mayfield?" Bill Sutter asked when she walked into Homicide. His skin color was even more pasty than usual. "I didn't hear that you've done anything to help advance our case. Oh, wait. You're sick. How could I forget?"

"What do I have to do?" she snapped. "Bring a note from my doctor?" She was irate, and unfortunately for Sutter, he was the only person nearby to take it out on.

A thin blue vein stood out in the center of his forehead. "You could have asked the medical examiner for one—she's a doctor. Oh, wait. You missed the autopsy, didn't you? Because you felt bad."

"But not nearly as bad as I'd feel if I let our prime suspect escape!" She marched to her desk, leaving Sutter with his mouth hanging open.

She sat and took a deep breath. "I'm sorry," she said. "I've had a bad day."

"Don't think you're the only one," he mumbled.

"Any surprises at the autopsy?"

He grimaced and shook his head. Bill Sutter despised autopsies and did anything he could to get out of attending one. They had become her responsibility in their "teamwork."

She really had no business antagonizing her partner. He had made a mistake, and so had she.

Ironically, they both managed to do the same thing.

They both lost Richie Amalfi.

Stupidly, she believed she and Richie had reached some sort of agreement to work together. After all, she chauffeured him around the city trying to find a reason for Meaghan Blakely's murder, as well as a possible suspect.

So much for trust. So much for being a complete sucker. She could have kicked herself, and that was nothing compared to what she planned for Richie when she found him again.

When, not if.

The fingerprint report had come in on Meaghan Blakely. Rebecca read that her real name was Meaghan Bishop, age 31, 5'6", brown hair, green eyes, 130 lbs. She had an arrest record a mile long in her late teens and early twenties for shoplifting, prostitution, possession, and selling. Then she either went straight or got smart, because the arrests stopped. With that background, Rebecca doubted it was the former. But considering the way she looked and was dressed, whatever she was into was much more of a "high caliber" crime than previously.

Whatever she was up to, it led to her crossing paths with a killer.

"I guess you saw this?" she asked Sutter, holding up the fingerprint report. He nodded. "Any luck finding where she lives?"

"You think I had time for that?" His voice dripped with petulance.

"All right, I'll work on it. Also, anything come in yet from CSI?" She rifled through the new papers that had been laid on her desk. "Did they find a second bullet?"

"What second bullet?" Sutter asked.

She realized Richie had only told her, not Sutter, his story. "Before you came in, Amalfi gave me his side of things." She gave him a quick run-down. "So Amalfi claims the gunman's first bullet killed Blakely, and the second bullet was the one that went off when he was wrestling the gun away—the one that might cause powder burns to show up on his hand if, that is, we had him here to test him."

"Sneaky bastard," Sutter murmured, rubbing his jaw where Richie had slugged him. "He only got away from me because we were being nice to him since he's almost part of Paavo's family and all. We should have treated him like the lying murderer he is! And no, no second bullet has been found, and isn't likely to be."

"Ah, here are ballistics on the gun."

"It's no help," Sutter said.

She read it quickly. The clip was empty. There was no telling how many rounds had been fired at the crime scene.

"Damn," she said. "You talked to the witnesses. Are they still claiming they heard only one shot?"

"The two bouncers as well as two gals who happened to be in the hallway headed for the Ladies' heard the shot. No one else heard a thing."

She stared at Sutter. "How soon afterward did they find the body?"

"The two women didn't know the sound was a gunshot. They heard a loud noise and went a few more steps down the hall. The door to Pasternak's office was open. They saw the body and raised holy hell. The bouncers were right behind them."

"Why were the bouncers out in the corridor and not at the front door or in the ballroom?"

"Probably because those two women are gorgeous," he said with a shrug as if it was the most normal thing in the world to abandon one's job to follow beautiful women.

She rolled her eyes heavenward.

A call came in from the dispatcher. A body riddled with gunshot wounds had been found in a car on Bayshore Boulevard near Oakdale Avenue. The next on-call team wouldn't take over for another six hours, so it was their call.

Sutter drove the two of them to the scene.

When they arrived, they saw that the car, an Audi A3, had been rammed into a building, its right fender crushed. The first responders had thought they were going to a single-car accident, a matter of a driver losing control, but when they saw the body and the car's interior, and pushed the body back off the steering wheel and air bag, they realized what had really happened.

As Rebecca studied the victim, a bad feeling came over her.

He was a white, middle-aged male, short, portly, well-dressed, and with two massive bullet wounds to the head. Skull, brains, blood and gore covered the car's interior.

Sutter put on his gloves, opened the passenger door, and took the car's registration out of the glove compartment.

"Mayfield, take a look at this," he said.

She walked around the car and took the slip of paper from him. The car was registered to Daniel Pasternak.

As soon as the Medical Examiner and Crime Scene Investigation teams arrived and moved the body from the car, Rebecca took the wallet from his pants pocket. The photo and description given on the driver's license matched that of the victim. It was Danny Pasternak.

Rebecca stood on the front steps of the Pasternaks' two-story Victorian in the Pacific Heights district and rang the doorbell. Officer Ray Dandridge, an eighteen-year veteran of the Northern station accompanied her. To approach the house where a murder victim lived without some sort of backup was never a smart move, so much so, that "Never-Take-A-Chance" Sutter made sure he always had something else to do.

In any case, Rebecca wanted to be the one to break the news to the new widow so she could gauge Mrs. Pasternak's reaction as she learned of her philandering, bookmaking husband's death.

Rebecca had been leaning towards Pasternak as the killer of Meaghan Blakely, or more correctly, Meaghan Bishop. After all, the shooting took place in his office, although Richie's description of the shooter hadn't fit Pasternak at all.

Who was she kidding? The most likely killer was the most obvious ... Richie Amalfi.

She shook her head at her foolishness. How many times had she interviewed friends of suspects, including some of the most brutal, heartless killers she ever encountered, and listened to statements about "what a nice young man" the killer was, and how "no one believed he could commit such a crime." Now, she held those head-in-the-sand beliefs.

She mulled over the statistics on murder cases. Over 80% were committed by someone the victim knew ... and Pasternak knew Richie Amalfi. But 16% of the time—one in seven or so—the killer was a family member, and of those,

40% of the time, the family member was a spouse. Since Danny Pasternak already had a mistress, to her mind, he would have few if any qualms about an affair with yet another woman. She wondered if he and Meaghan Bishop were an item. But, if so, why would she go to Big Caesar's with Richie? To make Pasternak jealous? That could be a motive for murder, but if so, who killed Danny?

No. She was clutching at straws, making up stories to prove Richie innocent when she needed to simply go where the evidence led her.

The deadbolt clicked, and the door opened a crack. One dark eye peered out. At the sight of Rebecca's badge, the door opened wider.

A sallow-skinned, middle-aged woman with sagging jowls peered up at her. The woman was five-foot three or four, wearing slippers and a bathrobe. Her hips and stomach were thick, and her breasts seemed to droop down somewhere around her waistline. "What is it?" she asked, looking from Rebecca to the police officer at her side. Her short hair was dyed auburn, but the dye job was yellowing, and a halo of grown-out gray glowed against her scalp.

"I need to speak to Mrs. Daniel Pasternak." Rebecca identified herself and her companion.

"I'm her—Barbara Pasternak," the woman said.

"May I come inside to talk?"

The widow didn't budge. "What's this about? It's Danny, isn't it? He's done something! Or is he hurt? Is that it?"

"I'd like to talk to you in private," Rebecca spoke gently.

Nervously, Barbara Pasternak invited her inside. As Rebecca entered, Officer Dandridge followed but stopped at the entrance to the living room.

The Victorian had been completely remodeled with walls torn out to open up the typically small rooms, and most likely to install new electricity and plumbing. This type of home, in this neighborhood, cost a few million dollars. Rebecca didn't think bookies made that kind of money.

They sat on matching high-backed, pillow-filled gold and orange chenille patterned sofas that Rebecca sank into and Barb Pasternak nearly drowned in. Rebecca faced her. "Do you know your husband's whereabouts this afternoon?"

Barb's bottom lip jutted out and she studied a pillow at her side, picking at unseen flecks or threads on it. "No."

"When did you last see him?"

"Yesterday." Her eyes went cold and hard. "He didn't come home last night."

"Didn't that worry you?" Rebecca asked.

She looked more bored than concerned. "No. It wasn't the first time."

"Any idea where he was?"

Barb went back to plucking invisible particles from the pillow. "I suspect with some woman. Not that it matters to me anymore. Why?"

Instead of answering, Rebecca asked, "Do you know of anyone who ever threatened him?"

"I suppose a lot of people," she said solemnly. "He wasn't exactly a popular man."

"Can you think of anyone in particular?"

"No." She rubbed the pillow hard, as if to smooth it, then stopped and cast a steely gaze on Rebecca. "Tell me what this is all about."

"I have very bad news."

Barb stiffened. "Yes?"

"Your husband was killed this afternoon. He was shot while driving his car. I'm sorry."

"Shot?" Barb half stood, then collapsed back onto the sofa. "Danny's dead?"

Rebecca waited for tears or hysterics, but there were none. Barb clasped her hands together so tightly her fingers reddened. "Who did it?"

"We don't know. We're looking for witnesses. We found him in the industrial part of Bayshore Boulevard. Do you know of any reason why he would have been out that way?"

Her eyes shifted. "No."

"Do you know about the woman killed in your husband's office last night?"

"Yes. Some detective called me. He wanted to talk to Danny. I gave him Danny's cell phone."

"Inspector Sutter?" Rebecca asked.

Barb nodded. "That sounds right."

"The dead woman's name was Meaghan Bishop. She was also known as Meaghan Blakely. Do you know her or know of her?"

"No." The answer was quick, curt, and angry.

Rebecca hurried on. "We're questioning several people in connection with her murder and Danny's. Did your husband ever mention anyone who might have worried him for some reason, or made him nervous about something?"

The woman's mouth tightened. "I don't know that anybody did that." She bit her bottom lip and dropped her gaze to the ground.

"We're investigating everyone who seemed at all close to your husband," Rebecca added. "How did he get along with people at Big Caesar's? The waitresses? Harrison Sidwell, the manager, the owner, members of the band and so on?"

"He never talked about any of them," she said.

"What about friends, associates? For example, Richie Amalfi?"

Barb Pasternak stared at the floor, then met Rebecca's gaze straight on. "He never spoke bad about Richie. They got along. But I still didn't like him!"

"Others you can think of?"

"He never talked to me about anybody he knew."

"I see," Rebecca said, standing. "Now, if you could accompany us to the morgue, we need you to make an identification. We'll take care of business as quickly as possible. Is there someone you'd like to call? Someone to be with you at this time?"

Barb shook her head, her jaw working as if she were grinding her teeth. Finally she said, "Let's get it over with."

Chapter 8

REBECCA PICKED UP Spike from Bradley's flat and then decided they could both use some fresh air, even though it was night. The backyard was small and cement covered with a square wooden planter box, about five feet by five feet, in the center. The wide edges served as benches. Rebecca sat beside a group of pink azaleas and purple petunias while Spike scampered playfully.

Bradley kept the flower bed weeded and the plants healthy. Rebecca's contribution was to keep Spike out of them.

Rebecca had decided to return home to get some sleep, good sleep, after escorting Barbara Pasternak back to her home. It had been a ridiculously long day, and she needed to be sharp the next day, Monday, as she put together the evidence on Meaghan Bishop's and Danny Pasternak's deaths. Logic told her the deaths were related, but she needed something substantial to prove it.

Unfortunately for Richie Amalfi, he wasn't with Rebecca at the time someone shot Pasternak. He could have murdered both people.

She took a deep breath as she petted Spike. The last twenty-four hours had been long and confusing on many levels. She probably needed fresh air to clear her troubled thoughts far more than Spike did.

She continued to pet her little guy. The vet thought he was a mix of Chihuahua and Chinese Crested Hairless. She had found him abandoned at a crime scene about six months earlier. He wore a collar with his name, but no other identifying information. She brought him to the pound, but weeks went by and no one claimed him. Rebecca feared a gas chamber loomed in his future because of his unfortunate "fur" situation—mainly his complete lack of it except for a tuft on the top of his head—and because he liked to bare his tiny but sharp teeth and to snap at everyone but her. Weird though he was, she took him home.

Although Bradley had a no-pets policy in her rental agreement, his heart went out—after he finished laughing—when she showed him Spike and explained the dog's situation.

Spike slowly grew to trust humans again, and stopped trying to bite anyone who came too close. She left dry kibble out for him while she worked, and cat-like, he only ate when hungry. When she was home, she fed him canned dog food or healthy people food, which he loved. She taught him to use a cat litter box, but let him use the yard when he wanted to. For a dog to use a cat's litter box had to be demeaning, and she didn't want Spike to develop self-esteem issues. Strangers pointing at him and laughing were bad enough.

He loved his home, loved her for saving him, and was a brave little tyke. She was surprised he didn't tear Richie Amalfi's throat out, come to think of it.

Bradley Frick stepped out onto the small balcony off his kitchen. From it, back stairs led down to the yard. "Rebecca," he called. "I almost forgot. I saw three strange men lurking around the building. They may have been looking for you."

"Why do you say that?"

"They seemed dangerous, like your police work."

"What did they look like?"

"It was too dark to tell, but they all looked big!"

She had a good idea who he saw. "Don't worry, Brad. They were most likely relatives visiting from Idaho."

"Oh, my," he said, his eyebrows high. "I'm not sure if that's a relief or not."

She thanked him for letting her know about the strangers, and went into her apartment with Spike.

Even though it was late, and she was tired, she took a long, much needed shower since she had missed one that morning. When done, she turned off the water and was reaching for a towel when she heard, "Just want to warn you before you come out, I'm ba-a-a-ack."

She froze. Wrapping the towel around her body, she stuck her head out the bathroom door and peered towards the living room. There stood Richie Amalfi, arms folded, head cocked, as he peered her way. He waved. She jumped back and slammed the bathroom door shut.

A minute later, he knocked on it.

"What?!"

"Here are your clothes."

She opened the door a crack and he handed her clean clothes, underwear included.

She all but threw on the jeans and a red ribbed turtleneck, then stomped into the living room. Her hair was wet, and she wore no makeup or shoes, but she didn't care. "How the hell did you get in here?"

He held up a keychain with a fob in the shape of the state of Idaho. "I found it in your sugar bowl. Really, Rebecca, that's way too traditional a place to hide anything."

"You searched my apartment? You went through my

things?" She wracked her brain ... of course, that first night when she was so tired she couldn't keep her eyes open. "You've got some nerve!"

"Don't worry. I found it the first place I looked."

She heard a sizzling noise at the same time as her anger quieted enough to realize that the delicious smells filling the apartment came from her kitchen area.

Richie hurried over to the range and flipped the steaks he was frying, then put salt and pepper on them. In a smaller pan, he was sautéing mushrooms. "I had a few things to check on," he said. "Then, I got hungry."

"You're a wanted man and you went shopping?" To her dismay, she was salivating simply from the aroma of his cooking. She hadn't realized how hungry she was.

"Actually, Vito picked them up for me. And my starving won't find the real killer any sooner."

She put her hands on her hips. "I don't know why I haven't hauled you in already!"

"Because you won't throw an innocent man in jail. Look, I didn't rig my own home to blow up, did I?"

"No, but you still have to prove your innocence to me."

He looked stricken. "I thought you trusted me."

"Like hell."

He opened the oven door and she saw French fries spread over a cookie sheet. She loved French fries. "Almost," he said, then proceeded to add a bit more butter to the sliced mushrooms.

Her stomach growled.

"Got any wine?" he asked.

"Look," she said, "I came home to shower, and take a nap. Maybe I ought to just go back to work."

"So? Do you have any wine?"

"No."

"That's what I figured." He took a bottle of pinot noir from a bag and handed it to her. "Want to open it?"

As she stood holding the bottle, he removed two salad plates with mixed lettuce and raw vegetables from the refrigerator and put them on the table with a bottle of ranch dressing. He found two dinner plates in the cupboard, and as she hurried to uncork the wine, he dished out the steaks, covering them with mushrooms, and then the fries.

Richie Amalfi, homemaker. Was she seeing things?

She also noticed that he no longer wore the wrinkled outfit, but had on a black pullover sweater and black slacks. On the sofa's arm lay a gray sports coat. He seemed refreshed, and even his hair seemed shiny and soft. She didn't like noticing such things about him, but reminded herself that she had been trained to be observant. Obviously, she couldn't help herself.

He put her plate across the table from his, then sat. "Wine?" he asked.

"Yes." Feeling awkward, she took a seat. "Thank you."

"Enjoy." He started eating. After a moment, she did as well, and found this all so surreal she would have thought she was dreaming except that everything tasted too delicious.

"So," he said, pausing to wash down the food with a gulp of wine, "What did you find out?"

She thought about the news she had to give him. He had told her he liked Danny Pasternak. "Nothing that can't wait until we've finished eating."

She had a good third of the steak left when someone knocked on the door.

Their gazes met. "You expecting Shay or Vito?" she asked.

He shook his head. "Is it a cop looking for you?"

She shook her head. "The door to the breezeway is

locked. And cops don't break in the way some people do! It's probably my landlord."

The knock sounded again.

Richie stood. "Be careful in case whoever's behind this is following us."

She nodded, picked up her gun, removed the safety and pressed herself against the wall as she headed towards the door. Richie moved to the area behind the door, his steak knife in hand.

"Who is it?" she called.

A sultry voice answered crankily, "Is me! What's wrong wit'chu, Rebecca?"

Rebecca relaxed. She knew that voice and that accent. Her friend, Kiki Nuñez, lived in the middle flat above her and below Bradley. She would have come down the backstairs to Rebecca's door. Now, Rebecca had two choices. Either try to send Kiki on her way without an explanation, or let her come in and meet Richie Amalfi.

Both were bad.

Rebecca managed to get Kiki to go back to her flat by telling her she had company—*wink, wink*—male company. Kiki's eyebrows nearly reached to her hairline as she took in Rebecca's damp hair and bare feet. Then she smiled, nodded, gave a thumbs up, and left. Rebecca knew from the look her friend gave her, that she would soon be doing some big-time explaining.

When she went back into the apartment, Richie had cleaned up a good portion of the kitchen. He pointed at the steak on her plate. "You want to finish that now or later?"

"I guess later."

He covered the steak with plastic wrap, and put it in the

refrigerator, then picked up the dishes and cutlery and loaded the dishwasher. He then reached for the frying pan he had used for the steak.

"Richie, wait," she said.

He stopped. "Yeah?"

"There's something you need to know." She waited until he put the pan in the sink. "There was another homicide today. A drive-by shooting."

He nodded. "I know. Danny bought the farm."

"You know?" Thoughts swirled about what that might mean.

"Don't get crazy on me, Rebecca," he said. He washed his hands then wiped them with a paper towel. "I got a call from Vito. You can't keep something like that quiet. That's why we're going to find Danny's killer." He threw away the towel.

She shook her head. "I've got to turn you in, you know."

"No, you don't." He walked over to the rocking chair and sat. "Besides, we could both use a good night's sleep."

Her jaw dropped. "You aren't suggesting—"

"I sure am. Where else do I have to go?"

"You can't—"

"I stayed here last night."

"But I was—"

"Yes?"

She shut her eyes. If word got out that she had fallen asleep with a wanted man in her apartment ...

"That couldn't be helped!" she said.

"No, maybe not. But other things ..." He lifted an eyebrow.

She hated it when he did that. "I have no idea what you're talking about."

"Rebecca, I've come to know you pretty well. Being

handcuffed to a person will do that. That means I know there's no way on earth you would give some cop your only handcuff key. You had one someplace near, ready to free you earlier today if things got dicey. Maybe in your purse. More likely, in your jeans, where it would stay hidden from me. No way in hell I'll ever get into them."

"Truer words have never been spoken!" She folded her arms, throwing him hard looks. "In my distress at your outrageous behavior, I may have forgotten all about the key."

"You? Forget something?" He got up and walked towards her, his voice soft. "I think you just wanted to see where all this would lead."

"As if you didn't? Shay could have easily brought you a handcuff key when he came to my apartment that first morning."

"Touché." He took a step closer. "You know I'm no murderer, and you know as well as I do that I can figure out who's behind these murders about a hundred times faster than that worthless partner of yours. You want my help; you just can't admit it."

"I want no such thing." She stepped back, increasing the distance between them.

He said nothing as the seconds ticked by, then he nodded. "Go get some sleep, Rebecca. You're raving."

He again sat on the sofa, used the remote to click on the TV. "I hope you don't mind, I have trouble sleeping in such a quiet place."

Despite herself, she didn't have the heart to turn him out of the apartment or try to strong-arm him down to the jail. She also couldn't help but think of him lying out here alone on that sofa, a sofa which was way too small for him.

Chapter 9

THE NEXT MORNING, Rebecca got up early while Richie slept with the TV still on, and Spike curled up at his feet—little traitor! She dressed and headed for Homicide to get some work done. Some real work.

She needed to run a normal investigation of the murders, the kind she had always conducted before Richie Amalfi upended her life. She needed to use foot work, computer searches, interrogations, surveillances, and everything else at her disposal, to find out all she could about her victims and potential suspects.

She started out on her computer. Meaghan Bishop had a three-year old California Driver's License that showed her living in Daly City, a San Francisco bedroom community. But she also had a Macy's credit card with recent activity that gave a San Francisco address. Well, lo and behold, Rebecca thought. Was that easy, or what? Finally, Rebecca felt good again about her investigation.

She went into the Macy's statements. Over the past seven months, Meaghan Bishop had purchased more than twenty-five thousand dollars' worth of upscale clothes, shoes and handbags. Each month she paid off the entire prior month's bill.

Just then, Lieutenant James Philip Eastwood, chief of the Homicide Bureau, marched into the room. He did not appear happy.

She found herself pinned back in her chair as Eastwood loomed over her. His anger about Amalfi's escape was bad enough, but his fury at not having been told about the escape and only learning of it after some reporters started questioning him, had sent him over the top. As he ranted, his face turned several shades of purple.

Apparently, the *Chronicle* had reported that a suspect had been placed under arrest on Saturday night, but when none showed up at City Jail, the press wanted to know why. Eastwood and the public relations officer, an officious woman named Isabel Hernandez-Kramer, who Eastwood hated even more than he did reporters, had to meet with them to explain.

Somehow, Eastwood managed to keep from the press the fact that the suspect had been let go "involuntarily." He claimed the man was merely questioned and released.

Finally, Eastwood stormed off making not-so-veiled threats about Rebecca's job if anything like that ever happened again under her watch.

She decided the best thing to do was to make herself scarce. She drove to the address on Bishop's Macy's account.

It was an apartment building in the Marina district, a location of upper-middle to upper class homes.

Rebecca introduced herself to the manager and owner. "I have a few questions about Meaghan Bishop."

"What for? Did you say you're in Homicide?" Mary Del Monico was middle-aged, overweight, walked with a limp, and had one clouded, possibly blind eye.

"As I said, I have some questions. How long did Ms. Bishop live here?" Rebecca asked. She had her game face on—no explanations, no reactions.

"Why do you say 'did'? Oh, my! She lives, uh, lived, here six, seven months now."

"Did she live alone?"

"She better! That's how I rented the apartment. No sub-leases or anything allowed."

"When did you last see her?"

"Some time last week, I'd say. What happened to her?" At Rebecca's stare, Del Monico answered the question. "She stuck to herself pretty much, not a friendly person."

"Did you ever notice any particular friends or family who came to visit her?"

Del Monico wrinkled her mouth. "I don't spy on my tenants."

"Maybe you happened to see someone—perhaps someone who helped her move in?"

Del Monico gave a heavy sigh. "Let me think. I remember one fellow. He was here a few times."

"Can you describe him?"

"I don't see so hot."

"Hair color? Build? Anything?"

"Black hair, maybe."

Rebecca felt her stomach drop. "Is he about my height? Broad shoulders?" She swallowed. "Kind of good-looking?"

"Hmm," she thought about it, then shrugged. "I don't think so, but I don't know. For all I know, I might have been looking at the garbage man."

"Well, if you remember anything more, will you call me immediately?" She handed the landlady her card.

Del Monico held it close to her eye. "I guess I could do that."

"I'm sorry to say, Meaghan Bishop was murdered. I'm conducting an investigation to find her killer."

The landlady's eyes widened. "Murdered? When?"

"Saturday night."

"My goodness." She pressed her hand to her mouth a moment. "I guess that means I'll have to clean out her apartment myself. I don't know if she has any relatives."

"You can't touch it until our investigation is completed," Rebecca said. "Something in it might lead to her killer."

"I can't touch it? Are you kidding me? How long's that going to take?" Del Monico asked.

"I don't know."

"But I have to rent it out! I need my rents to live on."

"We'll release it as soon as possible. I'd like to see the apartment now," Rebecca said.

Del Monico's small mouth tightened. "Do you have a warrant?"

"No, but as I said, Meaghan Bishop was murdered."

The landlady squared her shoulders. "That doesn't matter to me. I need something—a piece of paper—to justify letting anyone into her apartment. Landlords have been sued over doing things like that, you know!"

"Getting an approval to search the premises will only slow things down," Rebecca pointed out. "And we will get one."

She firmly raised her chin. "I need to protect myself."

Rebecca studied the woman. "We haven't met anyone not involved in the case who knew her ... until now. Will you come down to the Hall of Justice to identify her?"

"Me?" To Rebecca's surprise, Mrs. Del Monico looked and sounded quite pleased by the request.

"That's right. I'll get someone to drive you to the city morgue, and then back home. After that, we'll get a warrant to search."

Since Sutter was still at his desk, Rebecca asked him to

meet Mrs. Del Monico at the morgue. She then called for an officer to transport the landlady.

Rebecca was quite glad to send the woman on her way.

Her next step was to return to her apartment. She wasn't sure if she wanted to find Richie still there or not. As she was walking to her car, her cell phone rang.

To her complete shock, the caller was Shay. And the information he gave her was even more surprising.

Chapter 10

THE KINDS OF THINGS people put on Facebook never ceased to amaze Rebecca. As a cop, she would never consider revealing about herself one tenth of the personal information people thoughtlessly posted about their lives.

Shay, she discovered, had a particular talent for digging through Facebook for data. He found a woman named Sheila Chavez who tagged a number of photos with the name of her good friend, Meaghan Bishop. Sheila Chavez also told the world she lived in Daly City. That made her easy to find.

Rebecca rang the doorbell to the small, cookie-cutter house. A dark-haired, dark-skinned woman opened the door. She was dressed in a grubby, oversized T-shirt and jeans with holes. "Sheila Chavez?" Rebecca asked as she showed her badge.

Chavez's dark eyes grew wide with worry. "Yes. What's wrong?"

"I understand you were friends with Meaghan Bishop."

Chavez nodded.

"I'd like to talk to you about her."

"Why? Is she in some kind of trouble?"

"Unfortunately, she's been killed. Murdered. We're trying to find out whatever we can about her life, to try to determine why anyone would want to kill her, and who that person might be."

"Oh, my God! I had no idea." Chavez put her hands to her face. "Poor Meaghan. I'm so sorry."

"Can we talk inside?" Rebecca said before any platitudes began. She didn't want to hear how wonderful Meaghan had been.

"Oh, shoot. Everything's such a mess."

Rebecca was always surprised by how quickly sorrow turned into embarrassment over not winning a Good Housekeeping of America award. It happened time and again in her investigations. "It doesn't matter. I need some information."

Chavez opened the door wide. Rebecca stepped straight into a living room filled with toys, dirty dishes, and magazines. "I haven't seen Meaghan in a year or so," Chavez said. "I have no idea who would want her dead."

The contact was more recent than Rebecca had anticipated. "We don't want to rule anything out. You may know more than you realize."

As Chavez turned off the TV, Rebecca pushed aside papers and toys on the sofa and sat down. "How many kids do you have?" she asked.

"Three. The two oldest are in school, and the youngest is taking a nap now. We've got to be pretty quiet so we don't wake him up."

"Did Meaghan have any kids?" Rebecca asked softly.

"No, unless it just happened. When we were close, some years back, her old man didn't want any." Chavez picked up a pack of cigarettes from the top of the TV, then went to a recliner and sat.

"What was his name?" Rebecca asked.

"She's not with him anymore. They broke up some time

ago." Chavez lit a cigarette. "Everybody called him Sonny Blakely. I'm not sure what his first name was." She took a deep drag, then held out the pack. "Smoke?"

"No thanks," Rebecca said. "Meaghan was using the name Blakely when she died. Were she and Sonny married?"

"I can't imagine. They split up over three years ago. I remember because it was right after my Javier was born. Meaghan came into the hospital to see me, but she should have been in the bed instead of me. They had a fight—a knock-down, drag out. She was pretty broken up. Emotionally, I mean. To me, she was lucky to be rid of him. He was a gambler—addicted to it, if you ask me—and a creep. One day on top of the world, the next dirt poor."

"What became of Sonny Blakely?" Rebecca asked.

"I don't know. After they split, Meaghan moved out of the neighborhood. Since I had a new baby, plus my other two, I didn't see her hardly at all."

"Was she working?"

"She worked downtown. Macy's. She got by okay."

"You said you hadn't heard from her for a while. Did you two have a falling out?"

"No—it's life, that's all. We parted as friends." Smoke hovered over the room as she puffed. "The last time I saw her, she was still plenty steamed at Sonny. She said he left her and straightened up. Oh, man, that pissed her off!"

"Was Sonny Blakely in San Francisco as well? Did she say what he was doing?"

Chavez flicked the cigarette ash, half in the ashtray, half on the floor, then shut her eyes a moment. "It's hard to remember. I don't think she said, only that he fell into a pig sty and came out smelling like a rose, or something like that."

"Do you have any pictures of Sonny, by any chance?"

"Me? God, no! Why would I...oh, wait! There may be one on my old phone. I keep buying newer models of iPhones, but I think I left some photos on one of the older versions. Let me look at it. I'll have to plug it in to recharge."

As they waited, Rebecca continued to ask questions, but learned nothing useful. Finally, Chavez picked up an older iPhone model and scrolled through the photos dating back over five years. Rebecca got to see a young, vibrant Meaghan Bishop in those photos. The woman was truly lovely, and Rebecca felt the tragedy of her untimely death even more.

"Here we go! I know Sonny was at this party," Chavez said. "My daughter's baptism. We had all our friends come over, and Meaghan insisted Sonny join her. That was when she still hoped to turn him around, get him to want to get married, have kids, you know. Unfortunately, a leopard can't change his spots, as they say."

She seemed lost in thought a moment, then continued, "Meaghan was a traditionalist at heart. A good kid."

"Except that she had a record," Rebecca said.

"So? Doesn't everyone? Or almost." Chavez grimaced, then returned to searching. "Meaghan always had big dreams, and with her looks, she should have been able to get just about anything she wanted in life. But then she fell hard for Sonny, and that was it. I warned her; all her friends did. He wrecked everything for her, wrecked her life. I don't know why she was killed, but I do know I'd try to find out if Sonny was somehow involved."

Rebecca nodded. She found it interesting how the process of searching for photos often caused people to remember many things that they either had forgotten, or hadn't really wanted to say, and all kinds of details often emerged.

"Ah! Here he is. Wait, let me see if the next photo or

two...yes! Look. This is him." She turned the phone towards Rebecca.

She could have fallen off the sofa, she was so stunned at what she saw. Staring into the camera, looking glum and sullen, his hair nearly to his shoulders, wearing a T-shirt, with a cigarette hanging from his mouth and holding a drink in his hand, was Harrison Sidwell—Big Caesar's manager.

Chapter 11

REBECCA CALLED HARRISON SIDWELL and asked him to meet her at Homicide. When he arrived, the tall thin manager looked even more nervous than he had the night of the homicide. She led him into the interview room.

"Mr. Sidwell," Rebecca said after turning on the tape recorder and making the opening statement, "why did you tell me that you didn't know Meaghan Bishop."

He rubbed his mustache as if to give himself time to think. "I thought you said her name was Blakely."

"I thought you said you didn't know her."

He eyed her through his black-framed glasses without answering, then his shoulders sagged. "Okay, I did know her, but it was a long time ago. I hadn't seen her in years. I was afraid that if I told you, you'd come after me. I swear I didn't kill Meaghan. I was once in love with her. She walked out on me, though. Said I was no good—and she was right. I wasn't. Losing Meaghan was terrible for me. But it woke me up, got me to straighten myself out."

"You changed your name," Rebecca said.

"Actually, I didn't. Blakely was my step-father's name. I borrowed it when I was growing up. I was born with the name Sidwell. It's what's on my birth certificate. I just went back to it, and dropped Blakely. I never liked the guy anyway. He was a loser."

"And the name Sonny?"

"Harri-*son*. Sonny. Get it? I'll tell you, unless your last name is Ford, Harrison isn't a name for a kid to live with. I went back to it when I started working at Big Caesar's as a waiter. Now, I run the place."

"How did you manage that?"

He shrugged. "I discovered I have a head for business. I started helping with the accounting and payroll, and when the owner wanted to go down to Florida to live, he trusted me enough to leave me in charge. I now make more money than I ever dreamed possible."

"Give me the owner's name and contact information before you leave today," she said.

"Sure."

She returned to her questions. "When did Meaghan discover you've done well for yourself?"

He shook his head. "I have no idea."

"When did you first see her after your break-up?"

"Last Saturday night when she walked into the club on the arm of Richie Amalfi. He introduced us. I was shocked to hear the name Blakely. I guess she wanted to let me know she was doing well, too, the way she was all dolled up. She looked like a million bucks, I'll tell you. But using my old name ... that was a shock. It told me she hadn't forgotten me."

"So you two never married?" Rebecca asked.

"No." His voice was flat, but it seemed to Rebecca that he was trying to hide a surfeit of emotion,

"Did she go to the back offices that night to see you, Mr. Sidwell?" Rebecca asked. "It seems you two would have had a lot to talk about."

He rubbed his temple. "I wish she had. I had been watching her, looking for a chance to talk to her if Richie left her alone. But he didn't."

"But eventually," Rebecca pointed out, "she did leave the ballroom. Did you follow her?"

"No. I was busy with some customers."

"Too busy to talk to the woman you had once been in love with?"

"You've got to understand, Meaghan was ... different. She was trouble with a capital T. I had to think about getting mixed up with her again, frankly. Finally, I decided to go out to the hallway and wait for her to come out of the ladies' room. At least, I assumed that's where she went. But then, almost immediately, Richie got up and walked out of there, too. It made me wonder just what was going on.." He paused as if reliving the scene. "I had just left the ballroom when I heard a shot. I saw the bouncers run down the hall and I went after them. The door to Danny's office was open...and I saw Meaghan lying on the floor.

"That's all I remember. I kind of fell apart after that, I guess, because everything else is a blur. I remember the bouncers telling me they had grabbed the shooter. I told them to hold him in my office until the police got there." He bowed his head.

"Why didn't you tell me this before?" she asked.

"I was shocked, confused. Sad. I was afraid if you learned about the kind of guy I was in the past when I knew Meaghan, you might think I could have done it. But I didn't! I would never harm a hair on her head. A part of me still loved her, even after all this time..." His voice gave out and he turned his head away, taking deep breaths.

"Mr. Sidwell," Rebecca said calmly, trying to give him time to compose himself. "You said Mr. Amalfi left the ballroom soon after Meaghan. Did you see a waiter, or anyone, hand him a note before he left?"

Sidwell thought a moment. "No, not that I noticed. I think he simply got up and followed her out of the room."

"Why do you think Ms. Bishop went into Danny Pasternak's office?" Rebecca asked.

He shook his head. "I know of no reason for her to do that. I don't think she knew Danny, and besides, he wasn't there that night. I think Amalfi made her go in there. They were probably arguing or something, and he killed her."

"For what reason?"

"You'll have to ask him. He's a madman. In the time I've known him, he's done all kinds of crazy things. I wouldn't put anything past him."

She didn't like hearing that, especially since it went along with the kind of reputation he had, although she had to admit the reputation was at odds with the man she knew. Could she be so wrong about him? She continued with her questions. "I've been told Danny Pasternak was a bookie, and that he was usually at Big Caesar's on Saturday night, but that Saturday, he wasn't there. Do you have any idea why not?"

"You've heard wrong. He was my bookkeeper. That's all. It's true he liked to hang out at the club with friends, and to drink and talk. I don't think he had a happy home life at all. But I have no idea why he did or didn't show up on any Saturday night, let alone last weekend."

Troubled by all she had learned, Rebecca returned to her apartment. The sofa where Richie had been sleeping was empty. That was good, she told herself. She was used to being alone. Besides, something about him made her nervous. Maybe because she simply wasn't used to having a man around any more. It had been a while since she'd dated seriously. An even longer while since she'd been in love. Or even, sort of in love. She sighed. No sense dredging up that old history!

Still, she wondered where he had gone off to.

She headed for the bedroom to change into something more comfortable, and froze in the doorway.

He was lying on the bed, on his side, under the covers. She stepped closer. He looked peaceful, warm ... inviting. He opened his eyes and looked up at her, and something in them darkened. She felt her mouth go dry.

"I don't believe you," she said finally.

"So I've been told," he rolled onto his back, and rubbed his eyes. The covers slipped down and she saw with relief that he wore an undershirt. He groggily sat up.

"You're in my bed!"

"Don't worry about it. I'm on my side."

"*Your what?*" Did his audacity know no bounds at all?

He frowned. "That sofa's narrow, so after you got up so early, I saw no reason for a perfectly good mattress to go to waste!"

She threw up her hands. "So you spent the whole day in bed?"

"What, are you my mother now?" He ran his fingers through his hair trying but failing to tame the unruly mass. "If you must know, I couldn't sleep last night. I couldn't sleep until after you left."

"I give up!" she muttered.

"Good! Now will you leave so I can shower, shave and get dressed? Unless you want to watch ..."

She turned on her heel and slammed the bedroom door shut.

Hearing him chuckle only increased her irritation.

"I know a place where we can get some useful information," he called. "Want to come with me?"

She still fumed, even though she wasn't exactly sure what had made her so angry, but finally she said, "Fine!"

She only hoped that when Vito did the grocery shopping the day before, he had also bought Richie his own toothbrush. And a razor.

The inside of The Leaning Tower Taverna on the corner of Columbus and Vallejo was so dark Rebecca felt blinded. Richie directed her past the bar to a small dining area. "You aren't seeing us here," he called to the bartender.

"I never see nuttin'," the big man called, his voice gruff.

She slid into a booth in the back corner, and Richie climbed in next to her, a bit too close for her comfort.

"I don't see you either, baby," a waitress said to Richie. She had appeared almost immediately, gave Rebecca a quick once over and then ignored her. Rebecca was finding that reaction from Richie's female admirers irksome.

"So, what'll you have?" the waitress continued, openly ogling Richie. "You hungry, babe?"

"Carbonara," he said, then turned to Rebecca and casually draped his arm over her shoulders. "You should try it. Best in town."

She stiffened, but then tried to relax, realizing he was putting on a show for the waitress. "Fine," she agreed with a nod.

"And salads, Italian dressing. Antipasto, and bring some bruschetta," Richie said to the waitress as his hand now caressed Rebecca's upper arm. "In fact, keep it coming until we say stop. I'll have a beer, too. Anchor Steam. Dollface?"

It took Rebecca a minute to realize he was talking to her. Another to stop thinking about the warmth of his hand on her arm and then to realize it wouldn't have been smart for him to call her by her name since word may have gotten out that the SFPD's only female death cop was investigating the murder at Big Caesar's. "Coors," she said through gritted teeth. "Lite."

Rebecca had never seen anyone get such fast service, and soon Richie drank, she sipped, and both ate. Every few minutes her cell phone vibrated. It was Sutter. She didn't call him back.

Richie told her as much as he knew about Danny Pasternak and she told him what Shay had helped her learn about Meaghan Bishop and Harrison Sidwell.

"I can't believe it," Richie said. "He did look at her kind of strangely, now that I think about it. But he never let on he knew her."

"I wonder why not?" Rebecca asked.

Richie shrugged. "It would have been awkward. I mean, he and I are friends. I even lent him money. Then, for him say to me, 'Oh, that broad you're with, she used to be my old lady.' I don't think so."

Just then, Shay slid into the booth across from them. He said nothing, but cast a sullen frown in Rebecca's direction. He wore a soft heather-colored plaid jacket with a green silk ascot. If Rebecca didn't know better, she'd think he was on his way to some exclusive afternoon tea.

"What've you got?" Richie asked, twirling the hot pasta onto his fork and then filling his mouth with it.

"I looked for a computer or papers at Carolina's with no luck, but she had Danny's cell phone and home phone number, and that opened up a world of information. The most interesting were calls with a reporter for the *Chronicle*,

Sherman Glickman. The guy covers sports. He used to be the beat reporter for the Giants, but developed some sort of phobia about flying so now he only handles home games. Looks like the *Chron* wants to get rid of him, but because he claims fear of flying is a disability, they can't fire him."

Richie looked skeptical. "You think he's the ghostwriter?"

Vito joined them and sat down next to Shay. Again today he incongruously wore a big gold pinky ring that look like it weighed a couple of ounces, and an old, bulky brown car coat that Goodwill might have rejected.. "Writing ghosts?" Vito's eyes bounced from Richie to Shay. "What you guys talking about? How many glasses you had already? Or is this some kinda séance? Where's the Ouija board?"

They filled him in on everything that was going on. "Hey, you know what's weird about that?" Vito asked, then answered his own question. "Danny used to say Richie was the only guy he knew who had enough brains and knew enough good stories to write a book. You know that, Richie?"

"He did?" Richie appeared strangely pleased, even touched, by the news. "He never told me."

"Yeah. He liked to repeat your stories all the time," Vito said with a nod, then gave a sad smile. Rebecca watched both men's eyes grow a bit misty.

"Most the time," Vito said with a sniffle, "when he'd tell me one of your stories, he didn't even get it that I was one of the main guys there in 'em! Hell, I coulda told him the story better'un he told me. Poor bastard. Do you think he killed the woman, and the wrong person found out and got even?" Vito shook his head. "Like Dante said, there ain't no greater sorrow than to remember a time of happiness when you're miserable."

Rebecca nearly choked on her carbonara. She swallowed

fast. "Dante?" she said, reaching for some water. "Like, Dante's *Inferno* Dante?"

"Don't ask," Richie advised.

"My Ma told me if I only read one book in my life, make it Dante," Vito replied. "So I did. He was one smart *goomba*."

Everyone looked relieved when the waitress interrupted Vito to give him a beer and a massive tongue-and-onion sandwich with fries. He took a melancholy bite.

Shay opened a small notebook from the breast pocket of his sports coat and returned to business without missing a beat. "The *Chronicle* reporter will be able to explain why he and Danny were so chummy." He ripped a page from the notepad and handed it to Richie. "Here's Glickman's home address, cell phone number, plus his phone number at the newspaper."

"Good work." Richie folded the paper and put it in his pocket. Rebecca kept her mouth shut. She certainly would have turned up this information as well ... in another week or two.

Richie continued. "A couple of other things. I always dealt with Danny one-on-one, but I heard he had a wire room—two guys, couple hours a day right before game times. I don't know about sheet holders. You guys know if he had any?"

Shay sat back; gambling and bookies were Vito's territory. "Far as I could tell," Vito said, "Danny was too particular about his customers to use go-betweens. He'd built his clients over the years and only dealt with big boys. Guys like you, Richie. Trust was important to him. No need to branch out, rely on others. Besides, that's where a lotta slip-ups happen."

Shay stepped in. "Even with that, his operation was plenty big. Probably two to three million gross. I wouldn't be surprised if the layoff wasn't in New York or L.A."

"Two or three million dollars?" Rebecca could hardly get the words out. She had no idea! She might not be familiar with the terminology they were using, but she understood money.

"He was a stand-up guy," Richie explained. "People trusted him."

"Why would he set you up, Richie?" Vito asked.

"I don't know," he murmured. "Maybe it wasn't him."

"Or maybe whoever did it simply wanted to confuse everyone, especially the cops," Rebecca suggested.

Shay leaned forward, looked at Richie, and folded his hands on the table. They were slim, smooth, and long-fingered with buffed nails. A Perrier with a lime twist sat in front of him, but he hadn't touched a sip of it. "We don't need her."

"We don't need her working against me, either. We're out of here." Richie slid out of the booth and dropped several twenties on the table, more than enough to cover all meals and tips. He stepped back to let Rebecca out.

Vito turned and faced him. "Where you going, boss?"

"To visit a reporter."

Chapter 12

SHERMAN GLICKMAN STOOD at the front door of his ground-floor apartment, one hand wriggling around in his pocket searching for his key, the other holding a paper bag from McDonald's. The apartment building, in one of the city's rougher South of Market neighborhoods, was designed like a motel. Two stories tall, all of its doors opened directly onto a walkway. Rusted and chipped wrought iron fencing along the upper floors matched equally decrepit fences on the lower that provided meaningless barriers between the front doors and the sidewalk.

The smell of urine grew stronger as Richie and Rebecca approached the building. Richie hated everything about it—it reminded him of some of the places he and his mom had to live in when he was growing up after his father was killed, the kind of area filled with homeless and squatters. Rebecca didn't seem bothered. He followed her and stopped when she did.

"Sherman Glickman?" she asked.

Glickman spun around. "Who are you?" he asked, his frightened gaze jumping from one to the other. He was about five-six, wearing brown corduroy slacks and a tan cloth jacket zippered all the way up to the collar. He was chubby, with a stomach so round it looked like he had a beach ball under his jacket.

Rebecca showed her badge. "Inspector Mayfield, Homicide. We want to talk to you about Danny Pasternak."

He turned ashen. "The guy who was murdered yesterday?"

She nodded.

"Me? Why?" He almost bolted. His eyes were gray and small, his glasses frameless, and his light brown hair long and bushy, as if he were stuck in the seventies or overly admired Bolshevik intellectuals. "I don't know anything about him."

Richie hung back to observe and let the Inspector do her job. "Can we go inside and talk?" she asked.

"Yeah, sure. But who's he?" He pointed his chin towards Richie. "Why doesn't he show his badge?" Glickman's voice had a squeaky whining quality that made Richie want to punch his face.

"He's a ... consultant," Rebecca said, then repeated, "May we go inside?"

"Oh?" Glickman still eyed Richie, while Richie returned the stare until Glickman turned away to face Rebecca with a small, forced chuckle. "Is this sort of like *Castle* on TV? What's he, a writer?"

"Sure he is," she said.

Glickman stepped back so they could enter the living room. Then she added, "He's also one of the murder suspects."

Richie could have fallen over when she said that.

"*What?* My God!" Sherman backed up so fast he bumped into his coffee table and tumbled onto it. Under his weight, the legs buckled and the table collapsed like a cheap lawn chair. The furniture in the room was lightweight, blond-colored wood with yellow and green plaid-covered foam pillows on the sofa and chair. Undersized end tables matched the now destroyed coffee table.

Richie decided he needed to make nice if this little chat was going to be productive. He held out a hand to Glickman. "Don't worry," he said. "I'm here, so I'm in custody, right? Sorry about your table."

"Oh ..." Glickman eyed the offered hand warily and managed to get to his feet without letting Richie touch him. He glanced pleadingly from his table to Rebecca. "You sure it's safe?"

"You're a reporter. Since when do you care if it's safe or not?" Rebecca's words sounded straight-forward, but Richie had been around her long enough to see disgust at the squeamish reporter fill her eyes. Richie could all but hear the words that she didn't bother to speak, *It's a news story, shithead!*

He couldn't take it anymore—not the twerp's demeanor or his not having the decency to take a hand when offered. "It's not us you should be worried about!" Richie carefully enunciated the words to make sure the idiot understood. "Do you have any idea who you're up against?"

"What do you mean?" Glickman backed up even further towards the sofa and when his calves touched, dropped onto it. He gawked up at them like a kid in the principal's office.

Rebecca looked around for a seat. There was only one chair in the room.

"Here!" Glickman said, jumping up and leaving the sofa to the two of them. "I'll move."

He scooted into the easy chair, still tightly gripping his Macburgers. Richie's eyes met Rebecca's and rolled upward.

"All right," Rebecca said as she and Richie sat on the sofa. "Let's start over."

"Start over?" Glickman cried, the burgers perched on his lap like a lunch pail. "Why isn't he in jail?"

Rebecca ignored the question. "You were writing a book with Pasternak, a book that could make a lot of people unhappy."

"Not me!" Glickman's voice rose higher and squeakier. If Richie ever had an earwax problem, it was gone now.

"Cut the bull," he said, disgusted. "We're trying to save your life. What did Danny plan to write in that book of his? If Danny was killed to keep him quiet, you could be next."

Glickman's eyes rounded as if about to cry. "Danny told me no one would know! It was a secret. He had me sign papers agreeing that we'd never tell. He wanted it to be his story, written by him. I was glad about the arrangement, frankly." A bizarrely sly expression filled his face as he asked, "Uh, how did you figure out who I was and how to find me?"

Who would ever answer questions like that? Richie thought. No wonder this twerp couldn't make it as a reporter. "It's not important."

"Sure it is! Since you found me, others could as well."

Richie nodded and smiled. "There you go!"

Rebecca gave him a look that should have wiped away his smile, but he was too pleased with himself to let it.

Glickman dropped the burgers on the floor and buried his round face in his hands. "I knew I shouldn't have gotten involved. Pasternak offered me some money up front, and then a big percentage of the net." He lowered his hands, and faced Rebecca, looking simultaneously lost and petrified. "How could I pass it up? Look at this place. My job's on the line. I needed the money."

"Tell us about the book," Rebecca said.

He picked up the hamburger sack again. "Do you mind if I eat? I don't like them when they get cold."

"Please," Rebecca said. Richie marveled at her patience with the schmuck.

He pulled out a small, basic cheeseburger, folded the paper wrapping exactly halfway down, and took a small, almost mouse-like bite. He seemed to chew with his front teeth, then opened the bun and removed a pickle. He leaned forward as if to drop it onto the coffee table when he saw the table on the floor. He paused, the pickle wedged between his thumb and forefinger. Finally, befuddled, he dropped it into the paper bag, then took another miniscule bite.

Richie was beside himself. He was ready to shove the stupid burger down Glickman's throat, paper and all.

"The working title was *My Life as a Bookie*," Glickman eventually said. "He was going to tell all, how the odds-makers work, the kind of money the big fellows can and do make, and why it's usually the little guy who gets shafted."

"Hold it. Just a damned minute!" Richie couldn't believe what he was hearing. Not his pal, Danny Pasternak. "When you say the 'big fellows,' you don't mean he was going to write about his customers, do you?"

"He wouldn't do that." Glickman bit and chewed again.

"You're sure?" Richie asked.

"I guess." Glickman studied his burger and slightly rotated it to the next spot he would eat.

Richie leaned back on the sofa, hoping to ease his sudden heart palpitations. He ran his hand over the back of his head as he pondered Glickman's words. Bookmaking was illegal in California, but at the same time, any winnings had to be reported to the IRS as "income." A real Catch 22. If Pasternak had planned to name names and amounts bet and won, the IRS could go after those people for back taxes and penalties, which could be a small fortune. Most people involved in gambling should have been aware that the Feds used tax evasion to arrest, convict, and imprison Al "Scarface" Capone.

And if Rebecca could find any evidence that Danny planned to put Richie's name in the book, she might decide that gave him a motive to off Pasternak. Damn!

"Some of the players lost a lot," Glickman continued. "But the big players get the inside track to help them win. The odds are adjusted so more of the little guys are tempted to bet on the other side since bookies need to keep the bets pretty even so they don't lose money. Anyway, with a little creative point shaving or running up scores, whatever's needed, the game ends up the way that makes the big guys happy, and keeps the bookies in business. And, as usual, the little guy gets screwed."

Glickman peeled away the paper and plopped the last little bit of cheeseburger into his mouth.

"You and Danny," Richie said, waggling his finger at Glickman, "you both knew that when you tell how much somebody wins, that if the IRS finds out about it, then those people get hit."

Glickman finished chewing and swallowing before answering. "Sure." He dug into the sack for another burger. He pulled it out and was carefully unwrapping the paper when Richie lunged across the small room and swiped it out of his hands.

Glickman froze, petrified.

"What do you mean, 'sure'?" Richie loomed over Glickman. Rebecca also stood, her hand on Richie's arm as if ready to stop him if he became violent.

"Danny knew it," Glickman cried, hands upheld as if to deflect a punch that didn't come. "All he wanted was to write a best-selling book. It was a good plan. Good for me, as well. Now, though, we both have nothing."

"Sorry, Sherman," Rebecca said sarcastically. His situation hardly equated to Danny Pasternak's.

"Thanks." Glickman just didn't get it.

Richie was momentarily speechless at the thought his pal Danny was so clueless. If word got out about the book, certain people could get the wrong impression about him and Glickman. People they wouldn't want to mess with. He shook his head then slam-dunked the cheeseburger back into the paper bag. "I suggest you give me your notes and get out of town," Richie said. "You don't want anything that'll give anyone the impression you might rat out some of Danny's customers."

"He didn't tell me anything about them," Glickman whimpered.

"What names did Danny give you?" Rebecca asked.

"None! We only met a few times, and he spent it describing how bookmaking works. I knew how guys placed bets, but I didn't know what went on after that."

"You sure you know nothing?" Richie asked, stepping closer to him.

Glickman cringed. "I'm sure."

"Split this area, Sherman," Richie advised, "before it's too late."

Rebecca handed the reporter her card and told him to let her know if he thought of anything that might help in her investigation into Danny's death.

Richie and Rebecca stepped out the door. As Rebecca shut it, Richie's gaze automatically perused the street. In an instant, his expression changed from stunned silence to alarm. "Watch out!" He lunged at her, and slammed her face down onto the walkway. He covered her body with his, his hand over her head while his face burrowed against her ear, neck, and shoulder.

A hail of bullets flew at them, cutting a line across the front door where they had just stood.

She reached behind her back for her gun, but Richie had already pulled it from her waistband holster. He fired back, and at the same time grabbed her hand and the two of them barreled down the steps and dropped behind a parked car, using it for cover.

When there was no longer return fire, the two of them peeked over the car's hood to watch a black Lincoln disappear down the block.

"It's gone," Richie said, as he helped her up. "You okay?" He kept an arm around her as he rubbed away the smudge on her nose where it hit the ground. Her heart was in her throat at their close call, and he scarcely looked phased by it. Plus, he was much too close for her breathing to go back to normal.

She pushed him away. "Give me back my gun!"

He looked stunned. "Here! And you're welcome!"

"A cop could shoot you for taking his or her gun, you know!" she said as she tucked it back into her waistband, more than a little chastened at treating him so badly after he'd very likely saved her life..

"At least that'd put me out of my misery," he growled.

Glickman's head popped out of the door. "What happened? Are you two all right?"

"We are," Rebecca said angrily. "But I've got bad news for you. Looks like someone doesn't believe you know nothing."

He glowered. "If that's the case, why were they shooting at the two of you?"

Chapter 13

REBECCA DROVE ABOUT three blocks from Sherman's house then swung into a parking space and turned off the ignition, her face red and flushed with fury. "This has gone far enough! I didn't mind playing along with you to see what I could find out, but that doesn't include getting shot at with no means of self-defense! We're going to Homicide. You're going to turn yourself in to be questioned properly. By the book!"

"No! Wait! If whoever is behind this is shooting at us, don't you want to know why? I mean, why target me? Or us? But I somehow don't think you were the one they were shooting at."

Her eyes narrowed. What he said did make sense.

"I suspect that whoever's behind this thinks I know something," he continued. "Maybe because I was friends with Danny, and I think Pasternak was killed by one of the guys he was going to write about. Maybe one of them had a connection to Meaghan Blakely as well."

"Meaghan Bishop," Rebecca corrected him.

"Whoever the hell she was, she'll lead us to her killer. I'm sure of it."

"I can do that just as easily without you," she said, arms

folded.

"Maybe. Eventually," he said, and then his gaze darkened. "But you can do it a lot faster with me."

"No! This has gone far—"

"Just another few hours? Come on, Rebecca. You know I didn't kill my friend. And why would I kill that woman? I hardly knew her! I even gave you back your Glock. We can work together. We make a good team."

"In your dreams!" She leaned back in the car seat.

"At least I'm now positive you believe me," he murmured.

She grimaced at him. "What makes you think that?"

"Simple. You've been armed for five minutes and haven't shot me yet."

Rebecca returned to the Hall of Justice after dropping Richie off on the corner of Van Ness and Pine where Shay was waiting for him.

When she walked into Homicide, she learned Bill Sutter was off somewhere, but no one knew where. She took a look at her desk. Nothing new. She went over a bunch of reports, did a few more computer searches, and soon the hour was late and she was tired. She headed for home.

"Wha'chu doing with such a hot guy, Rebecca?" Kiki Nunez called from her back balcony. Rebecca had just entered the yard on her way to her apartment. "Wait there! I'm coming down."

Rebecca waited. What was Kiki talking about?

Kiki hurried down the back stairs, her high-heeled red mules loudly clacking against the steps. She was in her late forties, outgoing, energetic, flirtatious, and twice divorced. She had two grown children, and owned a classy spa in downtown San Francisco. How she managed to not only keep, but grow a wealthy clientele despite her flaming dyed red hair and too-tight outfits—quite the opposite of the style of her customers—Rebecca would never understand. But Kiki had the type of personality that was fun to be around. She was born in the US and spoke flawless American English, but loved using an accent at times, claiming it made her more interesting—especially to men. She liked all men. Young, old, big, small, handsome or homely, Kiki always found something to appreciate.

"What hot guy?" Rebecca asked, expecting to hear a description of Shay. He was the only person she could think of that might be considered 'hot' until, as Richie said, one got to know him.

"Finally, I got to see your mystery man! He was here just a little while ago looking for you, so I invited him up to my place for some wine. It's cold outside!"

"You invited him in?" Rebecca was appalled. "I've warned you that some of the people looking for me could be trouble! You never know when it's someone who has a grudge, or wants to get even with me for an arrest! You shouldn't do anything like that!"

"Relax, Becca! It was no problem. I looked in his eyes. They're so dreamy. Dark, deep, so sexy—"

Uh oh...Shay's eyes were blue.

"And his hair—"

Please say blond.

"Black as night, soft, wavy. And his shoulders!" Kiki spread her hands wide. "So broad and strong." She slowly lowered her hands, then raised her eyebrows. "And his—"

"Did he tell you his name?" Rebecca quickly interrupted.

She wasn't sure where Kiki was going, and didn't want to know.

Kiki shook her head and shrugged. "No. He said it's a secret. That you would be mad if he told me. Okay, I don't care." She put her hands on her wide hips. "I'll just call him Casanova. So, who is this Casanova, Rebecca? Why the big secret?"

"He's involved in a case. That's all. Nothing more."

"No?" Her eyebrows rose even higher. "He spent the night in your apartment, didn't he? Or most of it, I know, until I fell asleep. You can't tell me you paid no attention to him when he was there."

"He's not a good guy, Kiki," she said.

"He's not? Why? What does he do that's so wrong?"

Rebecca thought a moment. "I don't know yet ... but I'll find out."

"Girlfriend, the way he talked about you, I think, with just a little encouragement—"

"No way!"

"He *likes* you, dummy!"

"It's not that way between us," Rebecca said firmly.

Kiki shook her head. "Becca, what I gonna do wit'chu?"

Rebecca smiled. It wasn't the first time she'd heard that from Kiki. "Would you like to come in for some coffee or a beer?"

"No, thanks. I know you're just getting home from work." The accent vanished as quickly as it had appeared. "You look tired. Maybe you should get some rest so you can appreciate that guy more. And *do* something about it! Talk to you later!"

With that, Kiki headed back up the stairs to her flat.

oOo

119

Rebecca unlocked her door and took one step into the apartment when she saw Richie sitting on the sofa, Spike on his lap, and grinning like a Cheshire cat. "The things one can hear just sitting in your apartment are truly remarkable, Inspector. Not a good guy, huh?"

"I can't begin to describe how despicable you are," Rebecca said, putting down her handbag and removing her jacket. "I thought I took my house keys away from you. How did you get in here?"

"I may have taken them back," Richie said. As she headed for the sugar bowl, he added, "Or had a duplicate key made. I can't quite remember."

"Great! Now I have to get my lock changed!"

"Or leave it as is." He walked to the kitchen area and poured a cup of coffee. She wondered how long he'd been there if he had time to brew a pot. "You never know when you might need my help."

"I sincerely doubt that."

"Oh, yeah, you've got Kiki and Bradley in the building." He handed her the cup, having learned she liked her coffee black. She was surprised, but gladly took it. "I can see Bradley down here fighting off bad guys. On second thought, no, I can't. Or maybe Kiki can talk them to death."

"Very funny." She sat on the sofa, tugged off her boots, then put her feet up. Richie continued to stand and watch her long enough for her to feel uncomfortable about him, particularly remembering all the things Kiki had said, and even worse, all she had implied. She sipped more coffee—it was hot and felt good going down. "Why are you here?"

He paced back and forth across the small room a couple of times. "Someone's watching Vito and Shay. I doubt it's the cops, so that means I've got some real trouble out there. But I don't know why." He sat in the rocking chair by the heater.

She realized the house was already warm. She didn't need to come in and spend twenty minutes freezing until the ancient heating system warmed her apartment up enough that she could take her jacket off. She had lived in places that got a lot colder than San Francisco, but those places also had seasons of warm and even hot weather. In San Francisco the chilly dampness wormed its way deep into one's bones and rarely ever let up.

"It's not the cops," she confirmed. "Sutter doesn't know about those two, and I'm not having them watched. Whoever it is has to be interested in you, maybe in why you haven't been arrested yet. I wonder if they've managed to follow you here."

"No. I'm sure they haven't. So far, this is the only place I know that's safe."

"Safe from who?" she asked. "That's what I can't come up with. Yesterday, was someone shooting at you, me, or Glickman? If you know, Richie, you've got to tell me!"

"I have no idea."

She didn't believe him for a minute. She finished the coffee and stood. "Fortunately, caffeine doesn't keep me awake. I'm going to bed."

He moved to the sofa and turned on the TV. "Night, Rebecca."

She stepped into her bedroom and when she turned to shut the door, she saw Richie's profile as he sat facing the television. Kiki's words went through her mind, and she couldn't help but wonder if she were a different type of woman—someone more like Carolina Fontana, or even the waitress at The Leaning Tower Taverna—if she'd be sleeping alone, again, tonight.

Chapter 14

REBECCA LEFT RICHIE sleeping on her sofa. This was getting to be a habit. She also fully expected him to crawl into her bed again. The only thing disturbing about that was the masculine scent on the sheets and pillow cases. To her dismay, she liked it, and he seemed to fill her dreams—although they weren't romantic dreams, but ones in which they were constantly running from one danger to another.

This was clearly no way to live. She obviously needed to find herself a sexy cop to have a torrid affair with. The last thing she wanted was to get into her bed and think about Richie! Of course, if torrid affairs were that easy to come by, her life would be a lot more exciting.

When she reached her desk in Homicide, the crime scene report on the rice bowl from Richie's house showed no fingerprints other than his. That meant, as Richie suspected, whoever trashed his house had used gloves.

The telephone records on Amalfi and Pasternak had also arrived.

She began with Pasternak's phones. The list, however, was way too short. The man was a bookie; he lived on the phone. Those weren't his only records. How was it that Shay could find Pasternak's phone records, while she, using a by-the-book SFPD request form, had been given this garbage?

No calls were found between Pasternak and Richie. The names she saw meant nothing to her except one, the *San Francisco Chronicle.*

She dialed the number, and got an answering machine telling her she'd reached the desk of Sherman Glickman, Sports Department, and to "Please leave a message."

She went on to Richie's phone list. It was a lot longer than Pasternak's. Two numbers came up most often. One was to a Vito Grazioso. The other to a number whose identification showed only as "Private." Not even her reverse directory had any information, and she ended up talking to supervisors at the cell phone company who issued the number. It belonged to a Henry Ian Tate, address unknown. It was Shay's number.

Something about his name bothered her. She looked down at it again. Henry Ian Tate.

Then it struck her. His initials: H.I.T., as in hit man.

Just then, Sutter walked in with a warrant to search Meaghan Bishop's apartment.

Rebecca and Sutter entered the beautifully and expensively furnished apartment. Bishop had to have money to not only live in this neighborhood, but to afford such high quality furniture.

Rebecca searched for anything that might give a hint as to Bishop's killer. She found an iPad. It wasn't exactly high tech, but if it had a GPS, they might be able to use it to track her recent movements.

She also found a couple of old cell phones which she put into evidence bags, but no new ones. Since she had old phones, a new one must be somewhere.

In Bishop's unopened mail she found a car insurance bill for a blue Toyota Prius. The landlady had told her the apartment came with basement parking. Rebecca took a quick ride down on the elevator to look for Bishop's car. It wasn't there. Now, she knew which car the police should look for.

She called City Towing since the car had likely already been towed due to overdue parking. They didn't have a record of picking up the Prius, but would search further.

Rebecca went back up to the apartment.

Sutter met her at the door and put his forefinger to his lips. He led her to the bedroom and the clock-radio. He had opened the back and pointed to a small black button-sized object.

As Rebecca watched, Sutter used a screwdriver and needle nose pliers to disconnect the wires and remove it. He put it in an evidence bag. "Who would want to bug Meaghan Bishop?" he said. "There's clearly more going on with this woman than we've been able to figure out yet."

"Whoever paid for this place might be the one who also bugged it," Rebecca said. "I see no indication that she worked or paid for all this herself."

"How many men bug their mistresses' apartments?" Sutter said. "I mean, if you can't trust your own mistress ..."

"If you say so."

Sutter shrugged.

"This is crazy," Rebecca said. "Who lives this way?"

"Only crooks," Sutter muttered.

She gathered Bishop's bank accounts, and saw that she had received nine thousand, nine hundred dollars every month for the past eight months. If she received ten grand, the government would have demanded to know where it came from. It seemed she received the money in a cashier's check with no identifying information.

She tried to find some income tax papers, but could not. Bishop had a driver's license, a Macy's card, and a bank account. Nothing more.

Shoes and handbags made by Ferragamo, Gucci, Coach, St. Laurent, and some expensive-looking brands Rebecca had never heard of, filled the closet. More proof of money.

Rebecca had already turned away when the thought struck of what often happened when she changed purses— which, given the state of her wardrobe, wasn't often. She would move everything important, but at the bottom of the bag she would find little notes and receipts that she didn't want to transfer, yet she also didn't want to toss in case something she needed to keep was there. Usually in a hurry, she would leave them in the bag to sort through later.

She wondered if other women did that.

She began going through Bishop's purses, one by one. Sure enough, she found receipts, cough drops, grocery lists, dirty tissues, clean tissues, but nothing of interest until she came across a hand-written note with only an address: 99 Spruce Street.

"I wonder what this is?" she said, bringing out the note to Sutter.

Sutter called the office to check city records for the address. "It belongs to a city supervisor, Mark O'Brien."

Rebecca was stunned. Why would Bishop have a supervisor's address?

Just then, her cell phone chimed. Caller ID told her it was Sherman Glickman.

"This is Inspector Mayfield," she said.

"We've got to talk," he cried. "I'm scared!"

"Where are you?"

"I'm at the restaurant by the windmill at the beach."

She knew the place. "I'll be there in twenty minutes or so." It wasn't far away, but with a stoplight at nearly every corner, traffic moved at a snail's pace through the city.

She told Sutter something came up, and left Bishop's apartment before he could ask what.

As she headed for her car, she called Richie. To her surprise, he wasn't at her apartment, but apparently investigating something on his own with Shay. He would meet her at the restaurant's parking lot. She couldn't miss Shay's Maserati.

Rebecca and Richie walked into the Beach Chalet Brewery and Restaurant together. It was located above the Golden Gate Park Visitor's Center that featured historic WPA frescoes from the 1930's.

Glickman sat at a corner table, hunched over a huge Reuben sandwich and a coke.

"Are you all right?" Rebecca asked as she and Richie sat down across from him.

He shook his head. His tan shirt and tan jacket matched the color of his hair, making him even more thin, pale, and monochromatic than the last time she saw him. Only his round, ruddy cheeks gave him color. "When I got home from work today, my apartment had been broken into. The whole place was trashed."

"Trashed?" Richie asked. "Or searched?"

"I don't know. Searched, most likely."

"Any idea who did it?" Rebecca asked.

"No."

"What were they looking for?" she asked.

He hesitated.

"If these are the people who already whacked two others," Richie said, "and they're now after you, you're in trouble. The only thing that might save you is if you level with the Inspector. This isn't the time for secrets."

Glickman looked from one to the other. He was scared. Very scared.

"It's not my fault!" he cried. That, Rebecca knew from experience, was the first sentence out of the mouth of a guilty man. "It's just that I think ... well, I'm afraid I didn't give you the whole story yesterday. But it all happened because I was having trouble at work."

"What kind of trouble?" she asked, her voice filled with phony compassion.

"I'm not getting anywhere working for the *Chron.* Newspapers get skinnier every day, even big city ones. I'll be lucky to have a job in a year. And anyway, I've always wanted to write a real book—a book filled with journalistic fact-finding. One that'll make people sit up and take notice. One that'll open the door to a real future for me."

Rebecca couldn't help but grimace. The last thing she wanted was hear his sob story about failed ambition or missed opportunities.

"Didn't I hear you're no longer writing on the sports page because you don't like to fly with the teams?" Richie asked.

"So?" Glickman's lips mashed together. "That has nothing to do with the price of tea in China."

Richie winced while Rebecca gave Glickman an encouraging smile. "You're right, Mr. Glickman," she said. "Please continue your story."

"I met Danny when I covered the 49ers," he said. "Danny wanted to know the inside word on players' health, attitudes, what the team was saying about their opponents—

all the stuff that might go into which team might win, and which might lose. So, I told him. When I gave him particularly good intelligence, he'd reward me. It was mutually beneficial, but nothing illegal. We became friends. Then, I started hating to travel with the team, and my intel started to disappear.

"One day, Danny came to me and said the IRS was breathing down his neck. He owed them big time. The only thing he could think of was to make a deal. He'd give them enough info for them to go after others, and with the kickback he'd get from that—they actually pay snitches—he'd get out from under his own bill."

"I can't believe Danny would do that," Richie insisted, facing Rebecca. "He liked his money, but he wouldn't rat out his friends."

"You may be wrong about that," Glickman said. "But you're right that he liked money, and that's what led to all the trouble." He then stopped talking to take a small, mousey bite of his Reuben. Rebecca could all but feel Richie's patience vanish.

"Come on, come on, Sherman, hurry it up!" Richie growled. "You think I got all day?"

"It's my habit to chew carefully so I don't choke."

"I'll give you choke, you little shit!" Richie said.

Glickman pushed the plate to the side. "I'll go back to it later. Anyway, Danny came up with an idea. He knew that once he ratted out his customers, he couldn't work as a bookie anymore, so he decided to write the book I described to you. He offered me twenty percent of his profit if I did the actual writing for him. I agreed."

Richie and Rebecca nodded, both waiting for the punch-line.

"But then, I met with Danny and he began telling me his

story. Well, I'm sorry. I know he was a friend of yours and all, but it wasn't very interesting. In fact, it was pretty damned dull. The only way to make the book interesting was to talk about the people who were Danny's customers, especially the ones who were crooks and mobsters. I could write a little bio about how dangerous some guy was, and then show the risk Danny took to work with him. The public loves that kind of thing. That, at least, could be an interesting story. But it also caused a big problem for Danny."

"Damned right," Richie muttered.

Glickman picked up his sandwich. "I'm so hungry." He took a quick bite of it.

Rebecca was feeling every bit as impatient as Richie. "What was the problem?"

He put the sandwich down and carefully wiped his lips with his napkin. "The people Danny should write about don't want any public attention, especially not from the IRS or anyone else in government, if you know what I mean." With that, Glickman waited until both Rebecca and Richie nodded to show that they knew the type of person he was talking about. People who were, euphemistically, said to be 'connected,' the type Rebecca believed Richie to be.

"So," Rebecca said, arms folded and leaning against the back of her chair. "I imagine Richie Amalfi was in Danny's book."

Glickman glanced quickly at Richie. "Actually, no. He said Richie was a friend. He didn't want to involve him. Also, Richie was just small potatoes compared to others he was naming."

"Gee, thanks," Richie muttered.

"Finally, something good about you!" Rebecca addressed Richie. "Your bookie loved you."

"Har, har." Richie glared at Glickman. "You going to give

us the rest of this saga, or just sit there?"

Glickman cleared his throat. "There's not much to say. I guess, somehow, word got out about Danny's book and his list."

"Got out?" Richie repeated. "How the hell does something like that just 'get out'? I can't imagine Danny went around telling people."

Glickman chewed his bottom lip. "I don't know. I was in a bar after talking with Danny. I was getting a bit nervous about how things were going. Danny was acting odd all of a sudden, and I was worried he had changed his mind. Maybe wouldn't pay me at all. Anyway, the bar was the one not too far from Big Caesar's. Let's see, what's its name? You probably know it. You've got to go a block over to Columbus, and then turn towards North—"

"Get on with it!" Richie was completely out of patience.

"Okay...well, as I recall, this guy came up to me. He was big, with tattoos on his neck and arms, and—I'm not usually one to judge—but he was fairly, I'm sorry to say, not exactly good looking."

"Who was he?" Richie could scarcely speak, his teeth were clenched so tightly.

"He wasn't the person Danny was going to name, but one of his men."

"Who was the guy Danny was going to name?"

"Teo Reyes."

"Reyes! Are you crazy? He's one of the biggest crack and coke dealers in the Bay Area!" Richie did all he could to keep his voice down, to not shout his irritation at the dipshit. "He has people whacked every day! How could Danny even think about putting him in a book? No wonder he was clipped!"

"Actually, I don't think that's it," Glickman said. "Reyes' man, Tomas was his name, just laughed. He said Reyes doesn't care anything about the IRS. That he figured out long ago how to neutralize them. But he said I needed to tell Danny that Mr. Reyes didn't like seeing his name in a book. That it would make him feel strange, like he should be dead or something. And Mr. Reyes didn't want to feel like he should be dead."

"I don't believe you!" Richie said.

Glickman pouted. "There was a witness, but I don't know his name. If I did, you'd have to believe me."

This guy's story was even crazier than Rebecca imagined. "Someone watched as you talked to a drug lord's hit man?"

"Hit man? You think that's what he was?" Glickman whispered.

"Tell us about your witness," Rebecca said, ignoring his question.

"This guy, a stranger, was sitting far from me. At the end of the bar, in fact. But he could see there was some sort of ugliness going on. After Tomas left, he picked up his drink and sat near me, saying it seemed I could use a friend. He needed one, too. He bought me a drink—a much needed drink, I must admit. We talked a lot about his troubles with his wife. We also talked about how I wasn't married, and then my job. I said I was hoping to make some money—but he saw the result."

"Did you have more than one drink with him?" Richie asked.

"Well, yes. But he was generous and enjoyed our conversation. He even said I was a big help to him."

"I'll bet you were." Richie ran a hand over his mouth, then frowned. "What else did you spill?"

"Nothing! The guy—oh, now I remember, his name was George—he kept talking about his wife, and buying more drinks. I nearly passed out but, before he called me a cab, we may have discussed how I was going to make some money and leave town."

Rebecca nodded. "Did you tell him about Danny's plans for a book?"

Glickman looked from one to the other before answering, then down at his sandwich. "I had to, to explain what had just happened, but I hid it in general terms."

"Did you tell him about the list of names?" she asked.

"Of course not! Not exactly. I mean, I didn't want to cause Danny any trouble!" Glickman's mouth opened and closed a few times.

"What are you saying?" Richie fairly snarled the words.

Glickman appeared ready to pass out. "I think he guessed that the names were stored someplace. He asked me if they were safely hidden, and we talked about how important it was to keep anything like that concealed. I remembered thinking he was right, which meant I couldn't say that Danny or I had the list. That wouldn't have sounded smart."

"So what did you say?" Rebecca asked.

Glickman glanced at Richie, his eyes wide and frightened. "I told him Danny gave it to a friend, a powerful friend, someone Danny liked and trusted."

In a voice so strained he could barely get out the words, Richie said, "A friend?"

Glickman nodded.

"Who?" Rebecca asked.

Glickman barely moved his hand, but his index finger slowly uncurled and he pointed it at Richie.

Richie lunged across the table, grabbed Glickman's jacket and lifted him out of his chair. Rebecca also jumped up, tugging at Richie hands until he let Glickman go.

"What the hell were you thinking?" Richie bellowed.

The two customers and the wait staff glanced over at the table.

Glickman scrunched low in his seat, his voice tiny. "I didn't think anyone would go after you! I mean, he was just a guy in a bar who was crying about his wife! How was I supposed to know?"

"Give me your gun, Inspector." Richie spoke through gritted teeth. "I'm not going to kill him, just kneecap him, so he won't go anywhere, and *won't cause me any more trouble!*"

Glickman took a long slurp of his Coke with the straw, his eyes big and round as they jumped from Rebecca to Richie.

"When did you tell your story to the guy in the bar?" Rebecca asked.

"Friday."

"The day before Richie's date was killed," Rebecca said. "Two days before Danny Pasternak's murder."

"And," Richie said, "the day before my house was tossed by someone *looking for something in it!*"

Glickman leaned as far back as he could from Richie. "Uh, yeah. I'd say that's right. But I'm sure it's not connected."

Richie sat, arms folded, glaring fiercely at Glickman.

"Where's the disk now?" Rebecca asked.

"It's actually a thumb drive," Glickman said. "But I don't have it! Not me!"

Like hell. "If you're writing the book, you've got to have a copy," Rebecca stated.

"But I don't. Really."

She kept an eye on Glickman as she took a notebook and pen from her purse and slapped it on the table in front of him. "Write down any names you can remember."

"Do I have to?" Glickman looked nervous and pale. "I really would like this to all just go away."

Richie stood up and loomed over him. "You little piss ant! You got my friend killed, my house nearly destroyed, and now you want to walk away!"

Glickman slid so low in his chair he was about to disappear under the table.

Rebecca tugged on the back of Richie's jacket. "Sit back down."

Glickman quickly scribbled down some names. He no sooner finished than Richie snatched it.

"Let's see," Richie said. "Johnny Huang. Great! Just great! His real name is Huang Lao-ming. He runs the Lo Fung Tong that started in Hong Kong. They've got their fingers in everything. Then we've got Teo Reyes, Columbian cartel cocaine and gun smuggler. Wonderful! We also have the top tort lawyer in the city, and a couple City Hall types."

"So if we pursue these people," Rebecca said, taking the list from Richie, "we might be offed by the mob—Chinese or Columbian, take your pick—or I could be fired by the city, or any of us sued and left flat broke by a lawyer. Nothing like gazing into the future and finding it bleak." She perused the list and was startled to see Supervisor Mark O'Brien on it. Meaghan Bishop had his address in her handbag, which meant, finally, she had found a connection between Bishop and Danny Pasternak. She needed to talk to O'Brien asap.

"This isn't good, Rebecca," Richie said. "Any of those people would want to keep the whole thing quiet, and some would do anything it took to stop Danny."

"At least now we know why your house was searched," she said.

With that, the two left Glickman to his sandwich, with

instructions to find himself a hotel and not tell anyone except Rebecca where he was hiding.

At the moment, he looked more scared of Richie than anything.

After leaving Glickman, Richie said he was hungry, but he needed time to unwind before eating. He drove Rebecca's SUV across the Golden Gate Bridge to Mill Valley where he knew several good restaurants. The town wasn't Richie's normal stomping grounds, or that of the SFPD, so he felt fairly certain he wouldn't be recognized.

As they drove, Rebecca told him about finding Mark O'Brien's address in Meaghan Bishop's apartment, and that meant O'Brien knew both Pasternak and Bishop. Was it a coincidence or something more? She also told him about the bug in Meaghan Bishop's apartment.

Richie nodded, filing away the information with everything else he had been learning about the murders.

They went to a small French restaurant, and Rebecca was surprised to find that, away from his current troubles, Richie could be a charming dinner companion. They talked about movies, TV, music, even politics, especially San Francisco's. Through the meal, she found he had a rather remarkable ability to make her laugh. She wasn't sure how. Most men she went out with—not, heaven forbid, that she thought of their dinner as a date—were stultifyingly serious around her.

The evening caused her to remember how she had spent the early hours of Christmas morning with him the first time they met, how he was fun and full of life, and how he had entertained her with stories about himself and his friends, stories of adventures so quirky and amusing that she laughed until she had tears in her eyes.

How had she forgotten all that?

Chapter 15

THE NEXT MORNING, Rebecca and Sutter decided to check out the relationship between Meaghan Bishop and Supervisor Mark O'Brien.

The two detectives drove to O'Brien's stately home in a quiet, wealthy neighborhood edging the Presidio.

Rebecca rang the doorbell and a woman answered.

"Is Mr. O'Brien in?" Rebecca asked as she and Sutter identified themselves.

The woman was a maid, and she led them into the living room. She lit the fireplace and they waited beside it until O'Brien entered the room. He could have been a political pin-up boy with his gray hair sporting a long comb-over, sprayed and shellacked to stay in place, plus enough wrinkle-erasing Botox to render his face as smooth and shiny as his hair.

"Inspectors," he said by way of greeting them both as he shook their hands with an iron grip. "What can I do for you?"

"We have a few questions," Rebecca said, taking the lead as usual. "Did you know a woman named Meaghan Bishop?"

He looked puzzled. "No, not that I recall."

"What about Meaghan Blakely?" Sutter asked.

"No. Why are you asking?"

"Both names were used by the same woman," Rebecca explained. "And she was murdered Saturday night."

"Oh, yes! That's why the name seemed somewhat familiar. Why are you asking me about her?"

"Your address was found in her apartment," Sutter said. "We're wondering why."

O'Brien blanched, then squared his shoulders. "Well, I certainly have no idea."

"We've also found another connection between the two of you," Rebecca said. "Danny Pasternak."

O'Brien looked from one to the other before saying, "Pasternak?"

"Your bookie," Rebecca said.

"I never—"

"He listed your name in a book he planned to write on his career as a bookmaker." As Rebecca said this, her partner gawked at her in surprise. She knew he would be angry that she hadn't told him anything, but she was still trying to figure out how to explain having learned about it.

"He did?" O'Brien's voice was small. "Isn't he the man the newspaper wrote about who was found dead? A drive-by shooting?"

"That's right," Rebecca said. "It happened the day after Meaghan Bishop was shot to death in his office. You, Mr. O'Brien, are connected to both of them."

"That's a lie! A scurrilous, slanderous thing to say!" O'Brien thundered.

"You realize," Rebecca said calmly, "it would be better if you told us what was going on rather than having this blow up in the news. If you can explain the situation to us, I would certainly do all I could to keep my information quiet. Sometimes the best way to keep things quiet is to work with the police so we don't go poking around unnecessarily. Such searches may, at times, turn up a hornets' nest."

He didn't respond, but he continued to glare at her.

"We're offering you a way to put this behind you. If nothing is there, that's great. But without firm knowledge of that, my colleagues and I will be doing all we can to find everything we can about your dealings with Danny Pasternak and Meaghan Bishop."

"Is that a threat?" he asked huffily.

"Of course not. It's a fact."

"Look, I didn't know Pasternak was a bookie. Yes, I gave him money, but I thought it was nothing more than an office pool."

"Except that it wasn't in the office," Rebecca added.

He looked furious and she knew she had just made an enemy—an enemy who could affect her career in the city's police department. "It was harmless! Everybody bets on football games. Hell, you'd have to arrest half the men in this city if you were going to go after all of us."

"What about the ponies?" Rebecca asked.

"Never! I did football pools, or what I was told were pools. Nothing else."

"Big money pools," Rebecca said, doing a little guesswork. If Glickman remembered O'Brien's name, she doubted he bet small.

"So? I have a lot of money. I need to make a game interesting, or why bother playing?"

Rebecca and Sutter eyed each other. Sutter nodded. Rebecca said, "Tell us about Meaghan Bishop."

O'Brien walked over to the window and he stared out in silence for over a minute. When he faced them again, his gaze jumped from one to the other. "I'm a married man, a city official. It wouldn't do for my wife or my constituents to hear lies about any relationship between me and a woman like her."

Sutter spoke. "What kind of a woman is that, Mr. O'Brien?"

O'Brien scowled at him. "A hustler."

Sutter and Rebecca looked at each other in surprise. Sutter said simply, "Go on."

"What the hell! One day, out of the blue, Meaghan showed up at my house, all wide-eyed about politics, like some sort of political groupie. My wife was out of town, and I let her in."

"Come on, Mr. O'Brien," Rebecca said. "You can't be so foolish as to let a strange woman into your house without knowing who she was."

"She said"—he gulped—"she said she was a friend of Danny Pasternak's, and that she wanted to talk to me about the city's park services. I was intrigued."

"To talk about the park service," Sutter said with a smirk.

"That's right! I was set up! Things moved fast. We met a few times. She had ideas, schemes, ways to make money, things I should 'invest' in. When I wouldn't go along, she started making threats. Finally, there were photos. She was beautiful, and I was flattered and stupid. When the photos came, so did demands for money. I told her and whoever sent them to go to hell. I was willing to give up everything before I'd let myself be blackmailed. I never heard anything more."

"Do you still have the photos?"

"No. I burned them."

"Do you know who sent them?"

"I can't prove anything, but I'm sure it was her and Pasternak. She tried to hustle me, but I'm sure he was the one who came up with some of the plans. First, there were plans for ways to move city money to the three of us, and then when I wouldn't bite, she wanted money for the photos—money to make them go away. I thought Pasternak was a good guy, despite his line of business. I found out I was wrong."

"Why didn't you do anything about it?" Sutter asked. "Why not report what was happening to the authorities?"

"Because I'd have looked like an old fool to have gotten involved with her in the first place. And damn it, anyone who thought that would have been right."

After leaving O'Brien's home, Sutter returned to Homicide while Rebecca headed for North Beach. She drove around Sakura Gardens searching for a blue Prius. In a residential area two blocks away, the car sat collecting a fistful of tickets. She called CSI to pick it up and go through it with a fine tooth comb.

Since she was in the area, she went back to Big Caesar's to speak with its manager.

"You knew he was a bookie," Rebecca said to Harrison Sidwell. "Don't lie to me again!"

Sidwell sat morose and pouting behind his desk; Rebecca sat on a large, comfortable chair facing it. "I didn't have any actual proof, but I'll admit I didn't look for any. In fact, I purposefully looked the other way. What he did on his own time had nothing to do with me or with his job here."

"Even a *Chronicle* reporter knew he was a bookie," Rebecca said. "How do you know he didn't use the club's phones to run his phone bank, or simply for collecting illegal bets?"

"I don't know, and I don't care!" Sidwell cried. He took

off his glasses and wiped the lenses with a Kleenex. He looked as if he had aged about ten years with all the trouble going on around him, and he seemed thinner than ever. "It was a sideline for him, that's all. I'll admit, if some of his customers came here, they were big spenders in a lot of ways. People like the woman's murderer, Richie Amalfi. I knew some of his customers might cause trouble, but I never expected murder!" He drew in his breath and in a shaky voice added, "I never used his services, and I didn't want to know about them. My hands are clean. If you want to arrest me for looking the other way, so be it. My lawyer will get me off very easily."

"What about the people who worked for you? They might not have been so prudent," Rebecca said.

He put the glasses back on. "The people who worked for me didn't make enough money to use a guy like Pasternak. He didn't bother with ten-dollar bets. Five hundred was the smallest he'd waste his time on. Or, so I've heard."

"And I've heard you like to gamble," she said.

"I did—too much. It was a sickness. I gave it up completely, which is why I turned my back on Pasternak's bookmaking."

"Okay." Rebecca had tired of the subject. "Tell me about Carolina Fontana."

Sidwell's left eye twitched wildly. He gazed at the ceiling as if it might have his answer, then said, "I heard she was Pasternak's mistress. I also heard Danny's wife knew about her and hated her—and Danny."

"What about Meaghan Bishop? We've learned she knew Pasternak. Considering your background with the woman, how could you not know that?"

"I didn't know it!" Sidwell cried. "Why should I? I told you I tried to ignore Pasternak's work and everything about it."

"Was Meaghan Bishop a gambler?"

"I doubt it, but to tell the truth, I simply don't know. Meaghan was into a lot of things when I knew her. She was always coming up with ways to get ahead, to make money. She had big ideas."

"I've heard her described as a hustler," Rebecca said.

Sidwell chuckled. "That's probably one of the nicer things said about her. She wasn't a bad person, but she always thought she had gotten a raw deal in life. What can I say? When I think of how she ended up, I guess she was right."

"Why do you think Richie Amalfi might have killed her?" Rebecca asked.

Sidwell's chin rose. "Money, most likely. Like I said, that's all Meaghan was interested in. Richie has it, so did Danny. It was a bad mix. I'm sorry for all of them."

"We tried to find the waiter—or anyone else—who gave Richie a note saying that Danny Pasternak wanted to see him the night of the murder, but we had no luck. Has anyone come forward yet?"

"None of my people talked to Richie. I believe he just made that up, that he followed Meaghan, pushed her into Danny's office and killed her. That's the only scenario that makes sense, given what we know about all this."

Rebecca drew in her breath. "So it seems, Mr. Sidwell."

With that, she again interviewed the wait staff and other workers. She had one bit of new information. One of the band members now thought he might have seen Danny in the club on Saturday night, but he wasn't sure of the time. Since no one else remembered seeing him enter or leave, she wasn't sure if she could believe the sighting or not.

But if Danny was there, he could have sent almost

anyone to give Richie a note, and then told that person to immediately leave the club. And since Meaghan knew Danny, she might have gone into his office to meet with him as well, perhaps to work on some scheme the two of them had cooked up.

If the band member was right, this was the first bit of information that backed up Richie's story. But it did no good if she couldn't find some hard evidence to prove it.

And she still had a problem. Since it wasn't Richie who killed Meaghan and Danny, who was it?

Chapter 16

AFTER HER MEETING with Sidwell, Rebecca returned to Homicide.

Inspectors Paavo Smith and Toshiro Yoshiwara, the week's on-call homicide team stood in the middle of the room with Lt. Eastwood, and filled him in on their latest case. A fire had broken out in some slum apartments south of Market. A body had been found in the apartment belonging to Sherman Glickman. The fire had started in that apartment, and arson investigators were looking into it. It was definitely suspicious.

"Did you say Glickman?" Rebecca walked over to them, stunned by the news. "Is the body his?"

"The body was burned so badly, it'll be tough to I.D.," Paavo said. "The neighbors said they thought he was home. They also said there was some sort of shootout in front of his place Monday night involving a man and"—he paused, quizzically eying her a moment—"involving a couple of other people. It sounds as if Glickman was involved in something way over his head. Why do you ask?"

Rebecca slowly released the breath she held as Paavo began to talk about the shootout. She hadn't yet told anyone in Homicide about her meetings with Glickman. She especially wanted to keep the knowledge away from Paavo because of his connection to the soon-to-become-a-relative, Richie Amalfi.

"I found his name on the list of phone calls Danny Pasternak made," she said. "I planned to question him, but hadn't gotten to him yet."

Paavo fixed his pale blue eyes on her. He clearly knew there was a lot more going on than she was saying, and had decided to keep her secret. He was a good guy, and a friend. Even though he was engaged to be married, he still made her heart flutter when he was near. It was pretty much his fault that other men never quite measured up.

She turned to Eastwood. "If Glickman's death is connected to my cases, the apartment fire might be more than arson. It might be murder."

Eastwood nodded. "I agree. You and Sutter take it. Do you think Glickman's job as a reporter could have anything to do with his death?"

Rebecca shook her head. "I doubt it. He was in sports and apparently close to being fired."

Eastwood eyed her with suspicion. "Hmm. Well, anyway, keep me posted." With that, he walked away.

Paavo gave Rebecca his and Yosh's preliminary findings. "Let me know if I can help in any way," he said quietly. She nodded in appreciation. He understood the problem she had with Sutter, but this was their case now. He had two others he was already working on.

"Paavo, wait." She dropped her voice so others couldn't hear. "What do you know about Richie Amalfi?"

"I hardly know him, but I find it hard to believe he's a murderer."

"Would you trust him?"

She could feel him studying her as if trying to figure out what she was asking. "All I can say is, he's been good to Angie, and helped us quite a bit in the past. I want to trust him."

"But?"

"He's hard to read."

She nodded. "Any idea what he does to make his money?"

Paavo smiled. "I doubt even Angie knows the answer to that one. He used to dabble in real estate when the market was hot, and I have the impression he got out and made a bundle before the housing bubble burst. Now, I think he's involved in 'transportation.' I can question what he does, but I have no proof of anything."

Rebecca nodded. That was pretty much where she was with Richie's activities. She thanked Paavo, and let him return to his casework.

She returned to hers, trying not to spend any more time pondering the question of Richie.

She had barely gotten started when Eastwood called her into his office.

He didn't invite her to sit, although he remained seated as he said, "I know I was hard on you the other day about not keeping me informed about this case. I have come to learn that much of the fault *that time* was not all on your shoulders. I hope we can get past this and I particularly want to know whenever something potentially sensitive—like the involvement of a reporter—is involved."

"Of course," she said, knowing that was as close to an apology as anyone ever got from Eastwood. Apologies didn't matter to her—they were worth nothing in her book. But Eastwood clearly was trying to clear the waters. "I'm sorry about Glickman, sir. I would have come to you if anything at all had turned up."

"Good. One more thing I want to mention," he said. "I've heard rumors that you've been seen with Richard Amalfi. I'm assuming such rumors aren't true. Although the investigation has expanded quite a bit, he's still, I understand, a suspect. I want you to be aware of what some people are saying. Such stories won't do anything to help your career with this department."

"Thank you for letting me know," she said.

"It isn't true, is it?" he asked.

"I know Richie Amalfi is a suspect. I know that if I were to see him, I need to make an arrest."

His eyes narrowed as he looked at her, then he nodded. "Good."

Rebecca and Sutter went to Glickman's apartment to inspect the crime scene and talk to neighbors—the ones who hadn't been forced to leave their own burned-out apartments—to find out if they witnessed anyone suspicious lurking about at the time of the fire. Sutter was astounded to learn about the drive-by shooting a couple of days earlier, and that the woman being shot at resembled Rebecca, and the man with her sounded a lot like Richie. Rebecca shrugged the news off, but Sutter eyed her with increasing skepticism.

Sutter decided to talk to more of the neighbors while Rebecca poked around the burned out apartment. Glickman's computer, much to her dismay, had burned into a charred, twisted lump of plastic and metal.

This destruction made little sense to her. Someone must have believed Glickman knew a lot more than he said he did.

His appliances still stood in the burned out kitchen. The

range was charred black, and when she opened the oven door, it fell off onto the floor. The inside was empty. The equally blackened refrigerator was small, with a single door and the freezer compartment inside. She opened the door to find that although the fire hadn't gotten inside, the heat had caused the food to spoil, plastic containers to melt, and jars to crack.

Inside the small freezer were a couple of defrosted TV dinner packages and ice trays. She pulled out the trays. On the bottom of one, covered with water, was a thumb drive. Eureka!

She took it out and prayed the water and heat hadn't destroyed it as she placed it in an evidence bag. She knew one person who was probably quite good at retrieving possibly ruined data.

She heard Sutter walk back into the apartment, and immediately stuffed the evidence bag in her pocket. *First I harbor a fugitive, now I tamper with the chain of evidence. Great career moves, girl.*

She would turn it in eventually, but first she wanted Richie to go over the list of names. She was pretty sure she'd learn more about the men on the list from Richie than she could after hours of research.

As she drove home, anxious to tell Richie all that had happened and to contact Shay for help with the thumb drive, she suddenly swerved into a parking space and stopped the car.

What was wrong with her? She had always done everything by the book and took pride in being that way. Even Richie knew it, as much as his calling her 'Rebecca Rulebook' rankled.

Now, she found herself rushing home, looking forward to sharing police information with a suspect and asking for help from someone who might be a hit man. Had she gone stark raving nuts?

She should turn around, drive straight back to the Hall of Justice and give the thumb drive to CSI. To do anything else was wrong. She could be fired for it. Hadn't Eastwood warned her once already?

And if she were fired, what would she do with herself? She hated the thought of not being able to go to Homicide each day and see what new, interesting cases turned up, to not spend time with her co-workers: Luis Calderon, Bo Benson, Yosh, Paavo, or even—she shuddered—Bill Sutter.

She put her finger on the ignition button, ready to start the car and head back to work when, from the side view mirror, she noticed a black Land Rover slowly driving down the block towards her. It had tinted windows, and looked exactly like one that she spotted behind her for the past several blocks. She hadn't worried about it because she was on 9th Street, a major thoroughfare in this part of town. The Land Rover she saw earlier had turned right at the corner.

The SUV passed her and turned right at the same corner.

If it was circling the block, she was getting out of there.

As she drove along 9th Street, she noticed that the Land Rover had parked at the intersection. She kept going, but a short time later, she spotted it once more, this time a couple of cars behind her.

She turned left. The Land Rover followed.

She sped up and zigzagged through the streets, using every trick she had learned in her eight years of police work on how to shake a tail. Finally, she succeeded.

She found herself in Chinatown. Worried about who was

following her, and relieved to be free of them for the moment at least, she cautiously made her way home.

When she opened the door, the delicious scent of Italian cooking filled the apartment. Richie was at the stove, stirring a pot. "You're home, good!" he said. He looked casual and at ease, wearing black slacks and a blue shirt with the sleeves rolled up to his elbows. A lock of wavy black hair fell onto his forehead in a perfect arc. "I cooked up some spaghetti and meatballs. I was hungry. Vito stopped by with food, including salad greens for you, milk, sour dough bread, butter, and a bottle of Mondavi's cabernet sauvignon. You're just in time."

She walked past him taking off her jacket, and putting her gun in a cupboard. "Can you get hold of Shay?"

"Why?"

"I've got Glickman's thumb drive."

He eyed her stance and put down the spoon. "What's going on?" He moved towards her. "Something's happened."

She rubbed her arms. "I believe Sherman Glickman has been killed—burned to death," she said. "A fire broke out in his apartment and, apparently, he was inside. The arson team suspects it was set. They're still working on it. I suspect someone wanted to make sure he'd stay quiet."

He slowly absorbed the news. "I can't say I'm surprised."

"Me, neither."

"He was an idiot, going around talking to people. If Danny was killed to keep him quiet, whoever did that wouldn't let Glickman live ... or anyone else the killer thinks might know something."

As she realized what he was implying—what might come next—her gaze snapped towards him. "My God."

Richie stiffened, his lips tight. "Yeah, that's right. Glickman tried to save his miserable life by putting some of the blame on me. So if they've gotten rid of Danny, and now Glickman ..."

Rebecca's heart pounded as worry filled her. "Someone tried to follow me as I headed home just now," she began. "I lost them, but Lieutenant Eastwood told me people are talking about seeing us together. I might have been followed to lead the killer to you."

He stepped closer, a tightly controlled fury in his eyes. "Are you okay?"

She nodded. "I'm fine."

"Sure?"

"Absolutely."

"Good." He paced, his mouth a harsh, thin line and his fingers raking through his hair, as he pondered the implication of Glickman's death, and of Rebecca being followed. "The question is, was it the good guys or the bad guys doing the following?"

"I don't think there are any good guys involved in this mess. You might not be safe here. If they find out where I live ..."

"I'll be all right. It's better if I'm here. It's not that easy to find or get into, and I'm not leaving you here alone if those guys do figure out where you live."

"It's too dangerous," she said.

"I'm not running. This has to end."

She put her hand on his shoulder, stopping his pacing. "It will. I promise. I'll find who killed Glickman and the others."

"Unless it was a gang," he said, turning towards her. She dropped her hand. "Teo Reyes and Johnny Huang's gangs don't leave evidence, and they could have fifty eye-witnesses, but none of them would dare admit to seeing anything. If that's the case, you'll find Glickman's murder all but impossible to solve."

"But—"

"Rebecca, you know how they are!"

"I don't care. I'll do whatever is needed."

"No!" Abruptly, he gripped her upper arms, pulling her close and looking her straight in the eye. "We'll figure out what's going on, who killed Danny and Meaghan. Once that happens, whoever silenced Glickman will know I wasn't involved. You can't go poking your nose around people like Reyes or Huang. You need to be absolutely certain you can take them down before you make a move. Otherwise, it's too dangerous. Not only for you, but for your partner as well."

She placed her hands flat against his chest as if to hold him back. She could feel his heartbeat. "My job is always dangerous," she said softly.

"Not like going up against these guys. Talk to your boss, old what's-his-name who struts around the office like a peacock. He'll tell you to back off. He doesn't want to end up at the wrong end of a Chinese or Columbian dartboard. It's not healthy. Trust me on this."

She was ready to fight this battle. But if she did, she'd have to go it alone. Neither Sutter nor Eastwood would back her, of that she was sure. Her gaze intense, she asked, "If I did go after him, would you back me?"

His hold tightened on her. "If that's your choice, you know I would."

She could feel herself being drawn to him, wanting to close the distance between them, but that would have been foolish for so many reasons. She forced herself to turn away. She hated it when he, who was all emotion and unfounded intuition, made her, who was the epitome of precise logic and practicality, feel like she was being irrational.

She took a few more steps, and rubbed the arms he had held. She hated when he made her notice his touch, notice it and like it. And want more.

Richie stared at her a long moment. He then called Shay, and afterward, poured them each a glass of cabernet. "Shay will be here in an hour or so. He'll bring his laptop and some special software."

"Good."

He handed her a glass. "*Salute*," Richie said, holding out his glass.

She nodded. "*Salute*." Their glasses clinked together.

As she sipped on the wine, her tension began to ebb ever so slightly.

"It's going to be all right, Rebecca," he said. "Trust me."

She couldn't help but think that was the problem. She did trust him. Probably way more than she should.

They sat at her small kitchen table. He had dished out dinner and now waited, watching her, as she took the first bite of spaghetti. "Oh, my God. This is really good!"

He chuckled. "Glad you like it." He also began to eat.

She ate a couple more forkfuls. "I can get used to coming home to your cooking. You're spoiling me, Richie."

"Why not? You work hard. You deserve someone to do things for you once in a while."

"I don't know about that," she said with a smile.

He drank down some wine. "I'm surprised you aren't married, or don't have a steady boyfriend. Are you divorced?"

"No. Never married."

"Almost?" he asked.

She dug into the pasta before answering. "I guess you could say that."

"What happened?"

"With the first, I was too young. Probably too innocent." She tried to shrug it off and continue eating.

"The first?" He gave her a small smile filled with curiosity. "Tell me about it. I'm interested."

Why not, she decided. "Well, I still lived at home at the time, on my dad's farm. It was a decent size, nearly four hundred acres. My boyfriend—I guess you could call him my fiancé since we and everyone else assumed we'd get married—anyway, he lived on the adjacent farm." She paused then, to make sure he was still interested.

He nodded, and waited for her to continue.

"While in my late teens, my folks separated, but didn't divorce. I stayed on the farm with Dad, and my younger sister moved to Boise with Mom. I guess Eddie liked the idea of marrying the daughter of a farmer—merging our lands, making good money, and all that. But after Dad died and Mom sold the farm, he didn't find me—a woman with no job and no home—nearly as interesting. Before long, we stopped seeing each other."

"Is that why you left Idaho?" he asked.

"Thanks to Eddie, I realized there was a big world out there. In time, I got up the nerve to leave everything I knew."

"I imagine it wasn't easy."

She smiled and drank a little more wine as she thought back on those days. "I was scared to death. I mean, I was a farm girl, raised with potatoes and pigs. What did I know about the world? I adored my dad, and to lose him and a short while after, to realize how things had changed with Eddie ... to say it wasn't easy is an understatement."

"That Eddie has to be the world's biggest jerk," he said

indignantly. "I hope you haven't been pining for him all these years."

She chuckled. "God, no! I'm long over him." He refilled her glass. "But being a cop doesn't make for an easy love life."

"So I've heard," he said, digging into the meal with obvious relish.

She watched him as he ate, wondering not only why he was asking, but why she was answering. Maybe simply because he seemed to be a good listener. "I dated quite a bit when I first got to the city, but it took a few years before I met someone I could trust enough to let myself get serious about. We dated nearly a year. But as time went on, it became clear that the closer we got, the less he could accept that I was a cop."

"What do you mean?" he asked.

"For one thing, I was close to my male partner back when I was a uniform. It's only natural when you ride together, and watch each other's back. But it bothered Will a lot. The relationship ended when I got shot trying to break up a domestic dispute. It was only a flesh wound, not serious at all, but Will said it was him or the job. I chose the job."

"You loved him, but chose the job instead?"

She thought a moment, then decided to be honest. "Guess it means I didn't love him as much as I thought I did. As for the job, it's the best job ever."

She half-expected some sort of disagreement from him. Instead, he nodded. "Do you ever regret the choices you made?"

She didn't have to think twice. "No."

"You love your job that much, do you?"

"At this point in my life, yes."

He nodded. "That's good. It's good to live a life with no

regrets." His voice sounded wistful. "You're lucky."

"I wouldn't go quite that far," she said. Then, not sure why she wanted to know, she asked, "What about you?"

"Oh, I've had plenty of regrets!" he said with a chuckle. "Let's clear these dishes. Shay will be here soon."

"Just a minute! That's not what I'm talking about and you know it." She helped him carry dirty dishes to the kitchen. "Were you ever married?"

"No." He started to load the dishwasher while she scooped leftovers into plastic refrigerator containers.

"Close?"

"Yeah, you could say that." He took off his platinum Rolex watch while he ran some hot, sudsy water into the pan he had cooked the sauce in, then took a nylon pad and began to scrub it.

"And?" Rebecca asked.

He paused a moment. "I was thirty-five. I waited a long time for the right woman. I'll admit, I enjoyed being single. But then, out of the blue one day, I met someone. Someone special."

Something about his tone of voice caused her to stop what she was doing. She almost didn't want to know, but at the same time, couldn't stop herself. Her voice soft now, she said, "What happened?"

His shoulders stiffened, and his hands paused. When he spoke, his voice sounded gruff and harsh, as if he was determined to get the words out, whatever it took. "Car accident. On the approach to the Golden Gate bridge. Deadly spot, that Doyle Drive. Lots of bad accidents there. All my life I had that fact drummed into me. It takes on a whole new meaning when one of the statistics is somebody you care about."

Damn. She hated that something like that had happened

in his life, hated it that she should feel such sympathy for him. "I'm so sorry, Richie."

He forced his attention back to washing up and scoured the pan until it was cleaner than it had ever been. "Yeah, me, too. It took a long time to get over that. Don't know if I have, or if I ever will."

"Were you engaged to her?"

He rinsed off the pan and put it on the dish rack by the sink, but then left his hand resting on it as he said, "Yeah, for all of three days before she was killed. Before that, I was afraid to ask, afraid she'd turn me down." He drew back his hand and looked over the sink, as if wondering what he should do or say next. He rested both hands on its rim a moment. "Now, I see that was stupid. We could have had a lot more time together as a couple, being happy."

She picked up a dishcloth and began to dry the pan. "It must have been horribly difficult to handle."

"Yeah, difficult."

He sounded irritated with her, irritated both at her questions and that he was answering them. The room fell absolutely quiet as he scrubbed the pot so hard Rebecca wondered if he'd put a hole in it. She said nothing, waiting. "If you really want to know, I drank too much, ate too much, and screwed around too much. No drugs, at least. I didn't do that. Somehow, Vito and Shay got me to stop. It wasn't easy, and definitely wasn't fast. They got me to drink less, eat the right foods, even go to a gym. I hate gyms. Guys like me, we don't go to gyms." He shook his head. "I'm still not sure how they did it. Or why they bothered." He put the pot on the rack.

"Maybe because they're friends." She picked up the spaghetti pot to dry it as his words, his sorrow and disappointment settled deep within her heart. "You must have loved her very much. Very deeply. In a way, you're lucky for that. Sometimes ..." she hesitated, but then realized he was being honest and deserved the same from her, "sometimes I think I never loved enough."

At those words, he glanced her way, as if surprised at such an admission and perhaps wondering if she meant to make it. She could feel his gaze on her, but she refused to meet it. He went back to washing up. After a while he said, "The best thing, if you ask me, is to make sure you don't get too attached to people."

She nodded. "I learn that lesson every day in my job."

He grinned. "Boy, what a pair of misanthropes we are!"

She gave him a small smile. "I'm glad you told me. It actually explains a lot."

He was taken aback. "It does?" He lifted the wine bottle and saw they had killed it. He tossed it in the glass recycling. "Actually, Rebecca Rulebook, your dedication to your job— that explains a lot to me about your life as well."

"Hmm ... my life is supposed to be a closed, well-hidden book, opened to me alone." She put the pots in the cupboard under the sink. "I don't know that I like this."

"I can keep your secrets," he said with a grin.

The dishes done, he washed the sink then spread the dishrag over the faucet to dry. "I do have to say, though, I understand your old boyfriend, Will."

"You do?"

"Absolutely. I'm with him. I lost my fiancée and she was a bank loan officer. I can't imagine being married to a woman who walks towards danger every day."

Just then, there was a knock on the door.

Shay unlocked it and walked inside before Rebecca even reached it. He looked from her to Richie as if noticing the odd vibe in the room, took in everything surrounding them, and without any change of expression, put his laptop on the kitchen table, and fired it up.

"Where's the thumb drive?" he asked.

Rebecca handed Shay gloves, put on a pair herself, and then removed the drive from the evidence bag. Shay studied it closely. He took some canned air and other implements to dry and clean it. Rebecca and Richie sat and watched him work.

Finally he plugged it into his laptop. It whirred, clunked, and then asked for a password.

"So far, so good," Shay said. "As I suspected, it's password protected. I'll run my software to crack the password. Hopefully, Glickman wasn't too clever when he set it up."

"Try ghostwriter," Rebecca suggested.

"You think he'd use something so simple?" Richie asked.

"Absolutely. He was more proud of working on that than anything else. I can definitely see him using it."

Shay typed it and the screen unlocked. He shook his head. "Damn! She was right."

With that, he perused the file. "It's an Excel spreadsheet. How low-tech can you get? Take a look at this, Richie. You know several of these guys."

Richie pulled up a chair to sit by Shay. He gave a low whistle. "They're the guys Glickman told us about, plus a whole lot of others—some are names, some only initials," he said to Rebecca. "But now, we've got dollar amounts, plus wins and losses, to go along with all these people."

"The monetary amount itself probably doesn't matter all that much," Rebecca said. "Often, it's the little nobody's who think they should be special who do the most harm in this world."

"True enough," Richie agreed.

Rebecca stood behind Shay and looked over his shoulder at the list. Her gaze zeroed in immediately on "R. Am." She was pretty sure who that must be. She could scarcely believe it when she saw he spent $75,975 on bets last year, but only won $47,338. "My God!" she muttered.

"What?" Richie asked.

"Nothing." She lied. "It's a long list, that's all."

"If these numbers are true," Shay said, "Pasternak had a problem. The IRS cares when a gambler doesn't report his winnings. They don't give a damn if a person loses, and you can't report a loss anyway."

"Looks like you're safe from the IRS, Richie." Rebecca pointed to the name she thought was him, and couldn't stop herself from grinning.

"Real funny." Richie glowered. "Most years I do a whole lot better."

"Right." She loved how men liked to brag, even if it was over something illegal.

"And remember, Inspector, using a bookie isn't illegal in California," he added.

"True, but being a bookie is," she pointed out. "We never did learn how Danny planned to get around that one."

"Maybe," Richie suggested, "that's why he talked to his mistress about going to Aruba."

"Anyway," Shay interrupted. "Looking at this info, Pasternak didn't have a lot to offer the IRS."

"Which means he could still be on the hook to them," Richie said.

"Right," Rebecca added. "And if Danny went ahead with his tell-all book, the main people who could be harmed by it were those who needed to keep their names clean. Men who didn't want the public to know they were involved in any gambling, let alone illegal gambling."

Richie folded his arms and glared at the computer screen. "In other words, men like the city supervisor and the hot-shot lawyer."

"And that would make Pasternak's book one big dud." Rebecca scanned the names again. "The names he had aren't big enough for him to make money on. They might be of some interest locally. But even here, how many San Franciscans are going to spend their money to read that a city supervisor gambled? Who cares?"

"It makes me wonder," Richie said, "if Danny didn't realize his best way to make money was the *threat* of the book, not the book itself."

"Blackmail?" Rebecca asked.

"Exactly."

Shay searched the drive for hidden and erased files, then made copies of everything. Giving a nod to Rebecca, she removed the drive and placed it back into the evidence bag, and then removed her gloves. "I'll give this to the CSI's computer experts in the morning," she said. "I'll do it before Sutter learns I didn't turn in the disk today."

"Good," Richie said. "I don't want you to do anything that might jeopardize your job. Especially not now that I know how much it means to you."

She just nodded, but couldn't help thinking of Lt. Eastwood's words to her earlier. Her job might already be in jeopardy.

Chapter 17

"CAROLINA FONTANA," REBECCA said, facing Pasternak's *goomar* the next morning in Homicide's interview room, "did you see Danny Pasternak on Saturday night?"

Instead of answering, Carolina said, "I didn't know you was a cop! I would have told you the truth, if I knew, but there was no reason why I should, right? I mean, why would a cop be with Richie? That don't make no sense!"

Rebecca hit the button to turn the recorder off, then backed it up to where the interview started. She thought Carolina would answer her questions without wandering into territory that Rebecca didn't want the entire homicide squad to know about. Clearly, she was wrong.

She restarted the tape, giving all the preliminary introductions once more. "Tell me about last Saturday night," Rebecca said, trying another approach. "Did you see Danny Pasternak?"

She pursed her lips. "He told me not to tell anybody."

"Why?"

"I don't know. But you really are a cop, right? I mean, since we're here and all, I guess this isn't another trick of Richie's right?"

Rebecca cringed. "This is no trick, Ms. Fontana. Please answer the question. Did you see Danny Saturday night?"

"I saw him, but he was nervous like. I never seen him so nervous. He kept saying, 'If anybody asks, Carolina, just say you don't know where I am, and you never seen me for a long time.' So that's what I did. I listened to him, like always."

Rebecca asked the next question with abrupt coldness. "How long was he with you?"

Carolina sat up stiff and straight as she answered. "He stayed that night, and then he left the next day when Vito called and said Richie was looking for him. He said if Richie could find him, others could as well, and then he split."

"Who was he afraid of?"

"I don't know."

"Where did he go?"

"I don't know."

"Did he say he'd return soon?"

"He didn't say nothing. He just split." Carolina's voice grew higher and louder with each reply.

"Was he worried that Richie was looking for him?" Rebecca eyes drilled into her.

Carolina swallowed. "I don't think so."

"Did he know Richie had been arrested for Meaghan Blakely's murder?"

"Maybe." Carolina twisted her fingers.

Rebecca's voice grew louder, more demanding. "Did he tell you someone had been killed in his office Saturday night?"

"I don't remember." Carolina's answer was whispered.

Rebecca leaned towards her. "Did he know about the murder?"

Carolina started to cry. "I don't remember! I don't know anything! How many times do I have to say it?"

"All right." Rebecca sat back and waited until Carolina calmed down. "What time did Danny arrive at your home Saturday night?"

Carolina wiped her eyes. "What time? Hmm...I guess it was about one-thirty."

"One-thirty? You mean, Sunday morning?"

"Yeah, I guess that would be. To me, it's all Saturday night." When Carolina put down her Kleenex, half of one of her fake eyelashes had come unglued. It now pointed upward.

Rebecca did her best not to look at the furry-looking thing. "Why did he arrive so late?"

"He works Saturday night so he can pick up bets for Sunday's races. During football season, that's the biggest time people place bets." Then her eyes widened. "I mean, you know he was a bookie, right?"

"So I've heard."

"Oh, yeah, I guess Richie would have told you."

Rebecca couldn't help but grit her teeth as she said, "*Everyone* told me."

"And we talked about it, didn't we?"

Rebecca rolled her eyes. The last thing she wanted was for Carolina to remember that afternoon.

Carolina's eyebrows lifted. "And you two were so lovey-dovey"—Rebecca smacked the Off button on the recorder—"you wouldn't even let go of his hand. I remember now. That was so cute! That was why I never, ever would have dreamed you was a cop. Not with Richie!"

Rebecca stood. "Thank you for your help, Ms. Fontana. I'll show you the way to the elevator."

She hurried Carolina out of the interview room to the elevator. She was tempted to say, "Don't call me, I'll call you," but doubted Carolina would understand.

oOo

Sutter found Rebecca as she headed to the coroner's examination room, five minutes before the autopsy on Sherman Glickman was to begin. He told her he couldn't view it with her because he had to talk to 'some' people at the nightclub.

"Sure you do," she said.

"I knew you'd understand, Rebecca."

She did; he preferred to talk to nondescript people from the nightclub, people rather like imaginary friends, rather than to watch another autopsy. Not, she expected, that he would have much to offer if he did.

Sometimes she liked him even less than she liked Richie Amalfi.

At times, even she felt that watching an autopsy was overkill, so to speak, and was glad she had missed Pasternak's yesterday. There was nothing new. Two gunshots to the brain were the official cause of death.

This autopsy, however, was a different story.

First, the disgust factor loomed large. Watching a 'normal' autopsy was bad enough, but watching the coroner cut through charred, essentially cooked, skin was beyond nauseating. After her first burn victim autopsy, she couldn't eat barbecued ribs for over a year.

She had to know, however, if Glickman's death was caused by the fire, or if someone had helped him along beforehand.

She walked into the laboratory off the morgue just as Evelyn Ramirez was about to start cutting. Rebecca stared at the burned body on the table. "I thought this was Sherman Glickman's autopsy," she said.

"That's the name I was given. Presumed victim, his apartment, probably his body."

"Wait." She stepped closer. The body on the table was downright skinny. "Sherman Glickman wasn't tall, but he was fairly chubby. Would being in the fire shrink his body?"

"The flesh hasn't decomposed very much. From what I can tell already, this man not only wasn't heavy, he was emaciated. Also, from nasal, cheekbone, and tooth structures, he may have been of African descent."

Rebecca stared at her. "That's not Sherman Glickman."

"It's not?"

"I've seen Glickman. I've talked to him. I wonder who this man is."

"I'll know more in a couple of hours," Ramirez said. "But even now, I can tell you, whoever he was, he didn't die in the fire. Judging from the condition of the skin, he was dead before the fire got him."

Rebecca watched the rest of the autopsy with interest. The dead man's physical condition, state of his teeth, hair follicles, stomach contents, and so on, indicated he was very likely a homeless man who died on the street, was picked up, and tossed into the building before it was set on fire. Unfortunately, the city had so many homeless, a lot of them did die on the streets, especially in Glickman's neighborhood.

Knowing Glickman, he might have set this up himself—found a body, or someone near death, and somehow got him to his apartment, then torched the place with the body inside so he could run and the people after him would think he was dead.

But also, someone else could have snatched Glickman, and that person left the dead man behind as one big red herring to make everyone think Glickman died in the fire.

With the fire destroying the crime scene, it was impossible to know which had happened.

After the autopsy, Rebecca went to CSI. They had towed Meaghan Bishop's car to the Hall of Justice garage and had finished combing through it. They found a cell phone, downloaded its contents, and had transferred a copy of the information to Rebecca's computer.

When she returned to Homicide, she saved the information to a thumb drive of her own. She still didn't like the thought of turning over evidence to anyone outside the department, but then, she didn't like a lot of what was going on in this case.

As the day wore on, she couldn't rid herself of the image of Richie Amalfi sitting hungry in her apartment. She stopped at a KFC and bought a bucket of chicken with potato salad and biscuits on the side.

Only after she was half-way home did the irony strike her: a crispy corpse and now, crispy chicken. She suddenly lost her appetite.

Rebecca returned to her apartment to find not only Richie, but also Shay. She wondered why she bothered to lock the doors since it seemed anyone could waltz in whenever they felt like it. Richie was on the sofa and Shay sat at the kitchen table with Spike on his lap, giving Spike doggie treats, one after the other.

She handed him her thumb drive. "It has downloads from Meaghan Bishop's cell phone."

For the first time ever, she saw Shay smile. He actually was startlingly handsome. He plugged in his computer.

"I've got other news as well," Rebecca said as she put the chicken and side dishes on the coffee table with plates, utensils and napkins. "Sherman Glickman wasn't killed in the fire." She told them about the autopsy. "So Glickman might have staged everything, or someone kidnapped him and made it look like he was dead."

"No, he staged it," Richie said.

"How do you know?"

"You found the thumb drive. If anyone got to him, they would have made him give it up. But they didn't. He left it, either hoping it would be destroyed, or more likely, since it was in ice, he planned for it to be found so whoever wanted it would stop looking for him. Which means, he thinks someone might have a way to get info on evidence the police have collected."

"Which," Rebecca said, "is usually all but impossible, but maybe not in this case considering the level of some of the men who could be worried about what's on that thumb drive."

"Exactly," Richie said.

Rebecca had to ponder this in more detail, but on the surface, at least, what he said made sense.

Richie grabbed a chicken leg. "So, if nobody killed Glickman, that could mean nobody's after me either. And that I don't have to hide here anymore." He took a big bite.

"We don't know for sure what happened to Glickman," Rebecca reminded him, putting some food onto her plate as hunger overcame squeamishness. "As for you, you're still wanted by the police. We probably would have released you by now for lack of evidence, but running away did you no favors."

"Yeah, and you're the one in charge of my case," Richie said, pointing a chicken leg at her.

Shay called out, "I've got news about Meaghan Bishop."

"All right!" Richie grabbed a napkin, then he pulled out a chair and sat. "Join us, Rebecca."

"She did get quite a few calls from wealthy, influential

men, as well as from Pasternak," Shay began after Rebecca slid a chair next to Richie and looked on. "But she also received a number of calls from burner phones."

"I'm not surprised by the rich guys," Richie said. "She knew how to pick up men. I had no idea she was anything other than an attractive woman I just happened to meet at the horse races. What an actress! She even got me to think she snubbed her friends just to be with me."

"Who were her friends?" Rebecca asked.

"I don't know. I didn't meet them. Come to think of it, I couldn't quite tell who Meaghan talked about. She pointed to a group of women far from us, and said I was more interesting."

"The male ego," Rebecca murmured with a shake of the head.

He shrugged. "Anyway, we watched a few races together. I won more than I lost, and she called herself my lucky charm. That did it. She only left my side to get her jacket and tell her friends she had run into 'an old friend.' Hell, she may have attached herself to those gals to set up a good story—and, it worked. What a scam artist!" He grimaced at his ability to be so badly fooled.

"Whoever she was working with sent her to meet you," Shay said. "Whether that was why she was killed, we don't know yet. I have a start, and I'll keep going, but now, I wonder if whoever was using these burner phones is the key to her murder."

"I'll see what more I can find out," Rebecca said as she stood. "I'll head back to Homicide."

"I'm going out, too," Richie said. "I've been cooped up so long I feel like the Birdman of Alcatraz. I'll get Vito to bring me more fresh clothes, and then I'll get out of here."

"Be careful. This isn't over yet," Shay said to his boss,

surprising Rebecca that he would express such a human emotion.

Rebecca and Sutter were at their desks, discussing the material on Glickman's thumb drive when a call came in from Kiki Nuñez.

Her friend never called her at work. "Kiki?" she said.

"Becca, I don't want to worry you, but something's wrong. Your good-looking guy ..."

Rebecca's breath caught. "What about him?"

"I was just walking out the door, I had a hot date, but I heard some strange shouts. It sounded bad, you know, so I peeked out at the alley. A black van had stopped in the middle of the street, blocking everything. I saw four Chinese guys beating up your friend and some older guy. Then they took your friend, shoved him in the van, and drove off."

"Oh, my God!" Rebecca said. Chinese—that could be Johnny Huang's gang. She knew about them from the Gang Task Force. They killed and maimed without compunction. "Did you see which direction they went in?"

"They turned left. But I did better than that. I got the license number." She read it off. "And the older guy is here with ice on his head. He's kind of cute, you know. But go help your friend."

Rebecca hung up, her heart pounding. She could only hope she wasn't too late.

Richie slowly awoke. He opened his eyes only to shut them again from a bright light in his face. He was sitting on a hard chair, his ankles bound to the chair legs and his wrists tied behind his back.

He opened his eyes just a little this time. Even squinting, the light was so bright he couldn't see past it to look his persecutors in the eye.

He tried to pull his hands free, and realized zip ties had been used on his wrists.

"We heard that you were going to write a book about us, Richie," a voice said.

"No way." He tugged hard on the ties, but couldn't snap them.

"Do not act smart with me! The book was about gambling, and to be written with our mutual friend, Danny Pasternak. Why are you trying to cause us trouble?"

The voice was familiar—soft, slightly accented, and the English a little too perfect. *Johnny Huang!* Richie gulped. The leader of a modern day Chinese tong was ruthless. He knew how to keep his men in check, and his enemies scared. Richie once had a conversation with Pasternak about the danger in making book with men like Huang, but Danny liked the color of his money—and the quantity of it. He said Huang was one of his biggest customers.

Now, Richie might have to pay the price. "Come over here, Johnny, where I can see you. You know I had nothing to do with Danny's book. The guy ghosting it was a slimy prick. He used my name because he was afraid to use his own."

"Why don't I believe you?"

Richie tried to wriggle his hands out of the ties, but they were too big, too broad. He could feel the skin tearing.

"What, you think I'm an author all of a sudden?" Richie said, trying to sound incredulous. "Do I look like a writer to you? Hell! The book is dead, just like Danny. Did you kill him?"

Huang didn't answer the question. "I know about the

Chronicle reporter. He told my man that you were the one who had all the information, a list with people and money amounts—that you were the one who knew everything going on, much more than him, and perhaps as much as Pasternak."

"Your man? So was it your guy in the bar with Glickman. Your guy getting him drunk."

Again, Huang didn't respond, but said, "You met twice with Sherman Glickman. He has a lot of information stored in that small head of his, information he will gladly spill when he's drunk, or scared."

"He's a liar!" Richie shouted. "And for all I know, he's dead. His apartment was burned up, and he's missing. Did you do it? Is that when you got him to tell you goofy stories about me?"

Huang gave a derisive snort. "I would not soil my hands. I had no need to. He told my man everything we needed to know—that you have the list, all of Pasternak's information. Now, I want it."

"I hate to break the news to you, but your 'man' is too damned dumb to realize Glickman would say anything to deflect danger away from himself."

"Is that so? Unfortunately for you, *Richie,* what Glickman said makes sense. I believe you want any information about other people that you can get your hands on."

"Knowing you believed that jerkoff, *Johnny,* makes me think even less of you than I already did!"

All Richie could make out against the blinding lights was a silhouette coming towards him. A hard slug to the jaw rattled his teeth and made sparks appear before his eyes.

"I want Pasternak's list," the voice demanded. "I want all the information you have about my gambling and everyone else's."

"Why should I care about your gambling?" Richie shouted when he got his breath back. "Frankly, I don't give a shit about you!"

"We do not like to take chances." The voice growled, deep and deadly. "And we do not like liars."

"It's over, I told you!" Richie insisted. "Danny's dead."

"Word is out that you are planning to take over his business." Bitterness hung in the air. "And that you will give the IRS or any other Feds who come to call anything you can to get them out of your hair, including information about me."

"That's a lie. I'm not taking over a damned thing," Richie shouted. "How many times do I have to say I don't give a damn about you or the Feds? Who fed you that crap?"

"I still don't believe you. Why is that, I wonder?"

Richie shut his eyes and turned his head away from the bright, brutal glare of the light. He opened one eye, trying to see in the darkness, away from Huang and the others, trying to get some sense of where he was, how desperate his situation might be. Right now, it seemed hopeless. He knew Huang's reputation, and feared that the best he could hope for was that any torture not be prolonged.

He saw a movement in the distance, but whether it was one of Huang's men, or Shay or Vito—or hopefully both of his friends—he had no idea.

"How the hell should I know?" He finally said in answer to Huang's question. This back-and-forth arguing disgusted Richie. He had never backed down from a fight, and wasn't about to start now. "All I know is, you're hiding back there with your men surrounding you. And I'm tied up. What's the matter, Johnny, are you scared of me?"

"Not scared, disgusted."

"It's your men who should be disgusted," Richie said. He decided to throw caution to the wind. If it was his friends out there, this would give them a chance to help. And if not ... so be it. "They see what a coward you are! They know you're nothing! Nothing but an asshole."

Huang barked orders in Chinese as he strode towards Richie, in his hand something that looked like a small blowtorch.

Richie clamped his jaw shut tight, his body tense as he waited. He had a good idea what was coming.

"*Police! Drop your weapons!*"

Immediately, a shot rang out. The lamplight popped and the room went completely black. He saw bursts of fire from gun barrels, heard volleys of shots fired in rapid succession, along with the sound of running footsteps.

"*Drop your weapons now!*"

Was that Rebecca? He thought it sounded like a hard, ball-busting version of her voice.

The darkness made him disoriented, and the shots and running footsteps seemed to be coming from all directions at once. Richie held his breath, expecting pain, expecting death. To his amazement, he wasn't hit.

But he was a sitting duck and needed to get away from the gunshots. He started to rock the chair, trying to tip it over, thinking he'd be safer if he was lying on the ground instead of up here at bullet level.

Rebecca's hand touched his face in the darkness. He hadn't realized how well he knew her touch, her scent.

She grabbed his wrists. He heard a ripping sound as she hurriedly sliced through the ties, then slapped the knife into his now freed hands. She ran from him, firing more shots, drawing return fire away from him. He cut the zip tie around his ankles, and dropped flat against the cement floor.

Only a couple more gunshots sounded, a few more footsteps, and then all went quiet.

He waited. He had no idea which direction to go in to find safety, or to escape the room. He still heard nothing.

"Rebecca?" he whispered.

She didn't answer.

She had saved his life and now ... "*Rebecca!*"

"I'm here," she whispered.

Relief filled him as he scrambled towards her voice. "Are you near? I can't see a damned thing! Where are you?"

"Stay still. You're close. I'll find you."

"Ouch! That was my finger you stepped on!"

She reached out and felt the top of his head. "Why are your hands on the floor?"

"Because I didn't know it was safe to stand up." He reached up and found her hips, then her waist, holding it as he stood beside her, and then continued to hold her. He couldn't help but wonder about her reaction if he dared move any closer, if he dared to hold her the way he had wanted to for a long time now.

"Now you worry about your safety!" She wanted to slug him for scaring her so badly, or at least to push him so hard he'd fall over. Instead, she touched his face, knowing it well, even in the darkness. "You damned fool." Her voice was husky. "Were you daring them to kill you? What the hell is wrong with you?"

"Hell, if I'd known you cared this much..."

She smiled, knowing he was doing his best to relieve her tension, her fears—and his own--by saying something light and humorous. "Fat chance!" She replied in kind. "Let's get out of here." She grappled for him in the dark, finding his chest, then arms, then his hand. He gripped hers tight, and she could feel his fear and nervousness over his close call. "I think we need to go this way." She took a couple of steps and walked into something that fell over with a crash. "Uh, oh. What was that? Something's wet on the floor."

"It smells like wine. You must have knocked over a bottle," Richie said. "What is this place?"

"The cellar of an empty warehouse in the old Bayshore district. Probably a place winos hang out."

"Winos who had the sense to run, even leaving a bottle behind, when they saw Johnny Huang's gang pull up. How did you find me here?"

"Kiki saw what happened," Rebecca replied. "Between the van's license, traffic cams, and your burner phone's GPS, I was able to track you."

"God, are we idiots or what?" Richie said as he stopped walking. "Cell phones have a flashlight. Let's use yours."

"Mine? Are you kidding? It's city-issued. No flashlight. What about yours?"

"It's not much better," he said, dejected.

"So much for that idea," she murmured, as they slowly crept in what they hoped was a straight line. "Vito's okay, by the way. Kiki's taking care of him."

"Lucky fellow. But wait a minute. Where's everyone else?"

"Everyone who?" she asked.

"Your back-up. You didn't come after Huang's gang alone, did you? You aren't suicidal."

"I was tempted to call, but then you'd have been arrested, and I would have been in really hot water with my boss. So, when I saw how that spotlight blinded everyone, I knew what I needed to do. I waited to hear as much as I could until it got too dangerous for you. I think I picked the right time."

"The right time? Are you crazy?" He sputtered and

thundered simultaneously, an achievement she hadn't imagined was possible. "It was so close I could feel the wings of heaven's angels around me."

"You? Heaven? I don't think so!"

They reached a wall. Both leaned against it in relief, side-by-side, shoulders touching. "Well, whatever," Richie said. "But we still have a problem. They might be waiting for us outside."

"I know. Maybe I really do need to call for backup."

Richie took out his cell phone, hit a number on speed dial and handed it to her. "Tell Shay where we're located. He'll clear the way for us."

She explained everything to Shay, then gave him back the phone.

"Now we wait," she said, thinking about Huang's men possibly lurking around nearby.

"We need to find a way to kill time," he murmured, his voice sounding deep and definitely sexy in the darkness. "Want a suggestion?"

Chapter 18

BY THE TIME SHAY arrived, Johnny Huang and his gang had vanished. Richie figured Huang expected police back-up to arrive and wasn't about to take them on.

Shay soon left, saying only that he would do whatever it took to convince Huang that targeting Richie was a big mistake. After looking at his eyes as he spoke, Rebecca didn't want to know what he planned. She might have to arrest him.

She and Richie returned to Mulford Alley where Richie pried Vito from Kiki's loving hands and sent him home to his wife to mend his bruised face and tarnished ego.

As he and Rebecca entered her apartment, Spike ran up to greet them.

"Hey, boy!" Richie picked up the dog, then hugged and petted him. "I never thought this homely little mutt would look beautiful to me, but he does."

"Speaking of which," Rebecca handed him an ice pack, "put this on your face. You're uglier than ever with all the swelling that's going on."

"Gee, thanks. I'm not sure, which is worse, Johnny Huang's fists or your mouth." He sat on the rocking chair with Spike on his lap and the ice pack against his bruises.

Rebecca turned on the heater, then watched him a moment. "That must have been scary."

His one uncovered eye peered up at her. "Scary? Freddy Kruger movies are scary. Zombies are scary. That was god-damned terrifying."

"Bourbon?" she asked.

"Double. No, triple. Neat."

She handed him the drink and poured one for herself as well. She had been in a shoot-out twice before, and one of those times she was hit. She understood the fear he talked about. In that pitch-black basement, she not only dealt with the dread of what each moment, each gun-shot, might bring, but she also relived the terror of those earlier incidents.

She put on the heater to warm the place up, fed Spike some presumably yummy canned dog food, and then sat on the sofa. Richie was still shivering, but not from the cold. They both drank down their bourbon a little too quickly. She poured them each another glass, this one to enjoy.

After a while she said, "We've been looking at this as participants rather than as cops. It's time to stop that."

"Right now, I'd say we are participants. At least, I sure as hell am one." Richie sipped the bourbon and tilted his head against the back of the rocking chair, still holding the ice pack. "What do you suggest?"

"Let's go back to where this all began, Meaghan Bishop's death. Were you set up or did you happen to be in the wrong place at the wrong time?"

"How can you ask that?" He faced her with dejection and disappointment. "Clearly I was set up. I was given a note to see Danny."

"If there was one, it disappeared. So who took it? And when? No one came into the nightclub after the shooting as far as we know, or left it—other than the shooter you saw climb out the window. If someone took it, that person was still in the nightclub when I got there."

"You're right! And I'm right that a note existed, which means someone *in the club* took it. And Danny, who's always there on Saturday night," Richie pointed out, "wasn't."

Rebecca thought about this. "We never did get an answer to the question, why wasn't he there? You and Carolina say Danny was always in his office on Saturday night. But that night, he wasn't. Why not? What did he know? There had to be a reason, but so far, we haven't come up with any. Also, Carolina indicated Danny was afraid of someone."

"If he was blackmailing people, no wonder he was scared. But don't forget," Richie said, "that he knew Meaghan Bishop. Also, when we talked to Carolina, she had already heard about Meaghan's death, and even that I'd been arrested. She's hardly one to watch the news on TV or, God forbid, read a newspaper. So who would have told her about it, if not Danny? And how did he know so much about it?"

"Okay, here's my theory," Rebecca said. "What if Danny was there Saturday night? What if Meaghan went to his office to see him and he killed her? Danny was desperate for money—that's clear from Glickman. He was working with Meaghan on some kind of scheme, or schemes, to swindle money from people. What if it all went wrong and he had to kill her? Since no one heard the first shot—and, yes, I do believe that you found Meaghan dead—Danny must have used a silencer on the gun. Then, he picked up the shell, took off the silencer and had someone go out and hand you a note saying he wanted to see you. Danny then escaped out the window."

"So, who did I fight with?"

"A second gunman?" she asked. "Or someone working

with, or for, Danny. Whoever he was, he wore a ski mask and waited for you. He got you to fire a gun, pushed you aside, and climbed out the window. Without the silencer, people heard the second gunshot and found you in the room."

Rebecca stopped, sure Richie would poke holes in her theory.

"No way. Too many people jumping out windows, for one thing," he began. "For another, Danny couldn't do it. He had stubby little legs and a huge belly. He'd have needed a ladder to get out the window and he'd have been like a turtle on his back on the other side. The gunman, though, was big—some four or five inches taller than me, big and bulky. And strong. He could have done it easy."

"Okay. Forget the first part, keep the second."

"I think you're on the right track," Richie said. "At least, you don't have me shooting anybody."

They both sat quietly, sipping their second glasses—generous doubles—of bourbon, trying to put the pieces together.

"What I also don't get is why Meaghan wanted to meet me?" Richie said, breaking the silence. "I understand it was probably some kind of scheme, but I can't imagine what."

"After you met her, who suggested going to Big Caesar's?" Rebecca asked.

"Well...it seemed to just come up." He thought back on that day, not even a week earlier, when Meaghan was alive, vibrant and beautiful. "We talked. She said she was having fun, and assumed I was going to be busy that evening, and wasn't it a shame. I said I was going to Big Caesar's to see a friend. As I've told you, I often go there Saturday night, hang out at the bar, and place a couple bets. She sounded interested, said she'd never been there, so I asked if she'd like to go with me. We went to dinner first. That was it."

"Do you often take women with you to Big Caesar's?"

He lowered the ice pack as he gave her a look that said he wondered what her question had to do with the murders. Still, he answered. "Not often. The dating game's gotten a bit old after all these years. But if someone interesting or fun comes along ..." He shrugged.

Rebecca understood. She felt much the same herself. "So she would have known that talking to you would give her a good chance of getting into Big Caesar's. Would you like some fresh ice?"

"No to the ice, it's making my face numb. But yeah, she could have used me to get into Big Caesars. Or she could have gone alone or with a girlfriend."

"But she went out of her way to meet you. The question is why." Rebecca rubbed her temples. "And, then there's Glickman. Heaven only knows where he is. Given that Johnny Huang's boys didn't snatch him, and Teo Reyes' guys seem not to care, we can be all but certain Glickman faked his own death. And now, he's still running."

"Good riddance! Half-ass little twerp." Richie's mouth wrinkled in disgust. "As long as there's a McDonald's, he'll be fine."

Rebecca nodded, still thinking. Then she said, "Someone clearly wanted to get rid of both you and Meaghan and came up with a plan to take care of two birds with one stone, so to speak. That's the only thing that makes sense. So, who or what is the link between you and Meaghan?"

"Nothing! I just met her!"

Rebecca put her head in her hands. "What are we missing?"

"I don't know, dammit!" Richie poured himself more bourbon.

At least, Rebecca thought, he wasn't scared or shivering

any longer. Even somewhat beat up, he looked good. Once again, her gaze lingered on him a bit too long. She feared this was becoming a habit. She forced her thoughts back to where they should be. "Let's start with the first murder. What do we know about Meaghan Bishop? She was once young, perhaps a bit wild, and in love with Harrison Sidwell."

"I still find that hard to believe," Richie muttered, staring at his drink. "A woman like Meaghan with a wimp like Sidwell? Impossible."

"He was clearly a bit tougher in his Sonny Blakely days, I've heard." Rebecca stood and picked up the bourbon bottle in one hand, her glass in the other, ready to pour, but then she glanced over at Richie once more and abruptly stopped. It was already pretty late, and he would surely be spending the night in her apartment again. She had no idea what effect the bourbon was having on him, if any, but she knew her two glasses were already making her find him a little too tempting. No, a *lot* too tempting. And if she drank any more, she might decide the best way to handle temptation was too give in to it. But that would never do. Not with him, in any case.

She put her glass in the sink and the bourbon back in the cupboard. She noticed his eyes following her as she did it.

"Anyway," she said, trying to get back to business as she returned to the sofa, "the two of them split up, and she worked at Macy's, But then, about eight months ago, she successfully blackmailed someone into giving her ten grand a month."

"I sure know how to pick 'em," Richie said woefully as his dark gaze met hers. She had never before noticed how long his eyelashes were, but she had often noted the strong, firm line of his mouth.

She studied her carpet until her breathing went back to

normal. "Okay, so she probably had nothing to do with the mobsters Danny was going to rat out, and her fling with the City Supervisor came to nothing." Rebecca faced him again. "By process of elimination, that leaves you, Richie, as her killer. You did it. Nobody's left."

"Har, har."

"Well, who else? Danny's dead, there's no reason to suspect Sidwell, and the owner of the nightclub isn't anywhere near," Rebecca said.

"They're the same person," Richie said, putting his glass down and resting his head once again on the back of the rocking chair.

"Who's the same? Same as what?"

"Sidwell."

"What do you mean? He's the manager."

"And he's the owner."

Rebecca stared at him. "No. The owner is Brian Shoemaker. We checked on him. I even spoke to him. He's in Florida and leaves day-to-day operations to Sidwell. I don't think he has any idea what's going on."

"He sure doesn't. The guy's senile." Richie rocked back and forth. "He probably doesn't even remember that he sold the place to Sidwell last year."

"Are you sure?"

"I ought to be. I'm the one who lent Sidwell the money to buy it."

Rebecca couldn't believe he was just now telling her this. She jumped to her feet and stood in front of him. "You're part owner of the club?"

He stopped rocking, and sat up straight. "What? I lent him money, that's all. I don't want any nightclub! Two hundred large, at a great interest rate. Five years, a nice balloon payment at the end of the time. I'm a businessman, remember? The club's a money-maker. I checked it out before making the loan. Sidwell will pay it off. Maybe early. In fact, after the publicity in the paper, you'd think fewer people would go there. Instead, it's doing better than ever."

She folded her arms. "You are kidding me, right?" She couldn't stop herself from seething. What was it about him that caused that reaction in her? "You didn't really withhold this from me all this time!"

Now he stood up as well.. "Withhold what? I told you I lent him money."

She wanted to explain that she had thought in terms of a hundred, maybe at most, a thousand dollars, not two hundred thousand! Fuming, she walked over to the kitchen table, then turned, her palms flat on the table top as she faced him. "Sidwell lied to us about his position in the club. Why would he do that unless it was for some important reason? Innocent men don't lie."

"I'm sure it was a misunderstanding." He slid his fingers through his hair. "I don't know ... maybe his nerves got the better of him. Sidwell's a good guy, a go-getter, but he's high-strung as hell. I tell you, he made Big Caesar's what it is today. Okay, he knew Meaghan, but he explained that to you."

Rebecca pondered this a moment. "Sidwell had control over the crime scene and could touch the evidence before the police arrived. Did you see him the entire time until the police got there?"

He didn't answer for a long moment. "No. No, I was hustled into his office by the bouncers. But you've got this wrong. It's hard to believe Harrison would harm anyone. He's a soft-spoken, cautious guy. Mousey. For cryin' out loud, the guy even felt bad when his bouncers caught me. He said he'd help me get the charges dropped."

She thought a moment. "Meaghan's friend, Sheila Chavez, said Sidwell had a serious gambling problem."

Richie frowned, then picked up his phone and called Shay. He asked Shay to see if Sidwell was on Danny's list of customers.

As they waited for Shay, Rebecca said to Richie, "You do realize, that the list Shay is looking at is dangerous for you guys to have. You almost got killed because Johnny Huang didn't like you having all that information on him. I want it back."

"I'd gladly give it to you," Richie said, "but it's on our computers. Tell you what, we'll erase the files. How's that?"

Even if she stood over them as they erased the files, she knew Shay could find and restore them in the blink of an eye. "Fine. Erase them. I'm going to trust you to do it."

Richie put up his right hand. "Scout's honor."

She pursed her lips. *Sure.*

Just then, Shay came back on the line. Richie put him on speaker so Rebecca could hear his answer. "I see someone listed as HS," Shay said. "It could be him, but the bets are bigger than Sidwell should have been able to afford."

"How big?" Richie asked.

"Let's see." Shay gave a quick run-through of month to month activities, and then, the bottom line. "At the time Danny died, this 'HS' was in the hole to him over a hundred-thirty thousand dollars."

"A hundred-thirty large? Son of a bitch! I always knew there was something sleazy about that guy!" Richie shouted. He looked a bit ashen as he faced Rebecca. "If he was using money I lent him to gamble, you'll be right to arrest me, because I'm going to kill him!"

oOo

Since everything Rebecca had to tie the murders to Sidwell was circumstantial or pure speculation, the next morning she filled in her partner and together they got a warrant to search Harrison Sidwell's apartment as well as his banking, phone, and credit card records.

He went from shock to indignation to a raging anger when the two detectives showed up to investigate. Rebecca came away with a list of his accounts.

His investment information was so complicated, she was afraid she was going to need an accountant to sort it all out for her. She had a better idea. She transferred copies of everything onto her laptop, and then took it home where Richie waited to hear from her.

"You might want to call Shay," she said as she set up her laptop and opened the files.

Richie looked at them. "Maybe not."

Rebecca sat beside him and was surprised at how much he understood about Sidwell's bookkeeping and finances. She reminded herself that he was a businessman ... of sorts. He never did explain exactly how he earned his money, and now she guessed she could add "loan shark" to his nefarious activities. When she ran checks on him at work—all quite legitimate since he was a suspect—she found a network of companies that were so intertwined they made her head hurt. But nothing jumped out as illegal.

"I don't get it," Richie said. "Before I gave Sidwell the loan to buy the club last year, my auditors went over its books in minute detail. They came up with it being not only a good investment, but a place with lots of room for growth. It wasn't the 'hot' club of the moment, because what's up one month is passé the next. His idea was quality, to create a club with a solid reputation. But now its profit margin has flatlined. What the hell is going on?"

Rebecca left him alone as he worked through the numbers, providing coffee and sandwiches from a deli a block away. Finally, he sat back and frowned at the screen. "Got it."

She sat by him again as he pointed out the problem.

"The nightclub is nearly in the red because the salaries he's paying out take every cent. Six months ago, Sidwell hired 'Michael Brown' for sixty-grand a year. Two months later, 'William Jones' came on board, same salary. They had social security numbers, all taxes were taken out of their salaries, and even W-2s were issued, but they were never scheduled on the job."

"What do you mean?"

"They're fakes," Richie said. "Sidwell set them up, paid employer taxes on them—that was the reason for their common names, it makes them a lot more time-consuming to check on. Then, he kept their salaries for himself. He could have cleared over a hundred grand a year on those two names."

Rebecca studied the computer screen as he explained further.

"If we put together Sidwell's actions with Danny Pasternak's file of his customer's wins and losses, we can see that Sidwell started betting about seven months ago. As his gambling debts climbed, he developed one fake name. He was able to pay off Danny fairly quickly, but soon got into the hole again. He was fifty thousand in debt when the second name showed up in his books."

"How could he come up with fake employees?" Rebecca asked. "Didn't anyone else pay attention to what he was doing?"

"Remember, he had been bookkeeper and manager, and then became the owner. No one questioned him. Danny was never really much of a bookkeeper, and everyone but—I'm sorry to say—you and your partner, knew it."

She grimaced.

"Sidwell started gambling again," Richie said. "Did he make up the fake names to cover his gambling, or were both the actions of a desperate man trying to get his hands on more money? Probably, no one will ever know."

"Wait a minute," Rebecca said. "Sidwell's first fake employee showed up six months ago. Meaghan Bishop started receiving nearly ten thousand dollars a month about eight months ago. What if Sidwell is one who was paying her? What if he realized he couldn't afford the amount she wanted, that she was bleeding him dry? As a former gambler, an addict perhaps, he might have turned back to gambling for a 'quick fix.' And when that got him into worse trouble, he embezzled from his own business."

Richie thought a moment, and then nodded. "That's it. Sidwell owed Danny and he owed me, and Meaghan Bishop was blackmailing him. He came up with a way to get rid of all three of us."

Rebecca high-fived him. "Now, we just have to prove it."

Chapter 19

REBECCA CONTACTED SUTTER and gave him the information she had up to this point. He agreed that there was enough to bring Sidwell in for questioning, with an eye to an arrest.

The two met at Big Caesar's but Sidwell wasn't there, nor was he at his apartment.

They asked around, but no one had seen him, or had any idea where he might be. They sent out a BOLO, a "be-on-the-lookout," for him and his red Miata.

As they left Sidwell's apartment, they agreed to meet at eight p.m. at Big Caesar's. The club would be open by then, and Sidwell should surely be there. In the meantime, Sutter headed to Chinatown for an early dinner, while Rebecca decided to return to Homicide.

She walked to her SUV, unlocked the door and was about to open it when she heard a voice behind her.

"Step away from the car, and don't make any sudden moves!"

She recognized the voice, and in the car's window saw Sidwell's reflection. He stretched one arm out, pointing a gun at her. He was alone. She took a step backwards and in one quick movement, spun to face him, grabbed his extended arm, and elbowed him hard in the stomach. As he gasped and doubled over, she smacked the arm she held against her knee, causing him to cry out in pain and his hand to open, dropping his gun.

She then twisted that same arm behind his back and was about to toss him to the ground and cuff him when she felt massive, gorilla-strong arms go around her body and crush her arms against her sides in a vice-like grip so tight she feared her ribs would crack.

Her assailant lifted her off her feet, swung her away from Sidwell and then threw her to the ground with such force it knocked the breath out of her.

She could scarcely believe the size and strength of the guy. She was struggling to stand, still bent over, when he grabbed the neck and back of her jacket and hurled her into the side of her SUV. She hit it hard and rebounded off, falling backwards onto the ground. Her head struck the asphalt, leaving her dazed.

Sidwell stood over her, gun in hand. "Meet Tommy," he said, with a slow, lazy smirk devoid of any humor. Gone was the mousey nightclub manager and in his place was a man still nervous, but determined and potentially deadly. "Remove your gun and slide it on the ground towards him."

Pain slashed through her skull as she slowly sat up and glared at the bruiser who had tossed her about like a rag doll. His enormous body had a bulbous, jellyfish-like appearance with beady eyes so vacant they suggested the intelligence of a slug. Long, brown-tinged teeth showed through a loose-lipped, blubbery smile that was almost lewd as he stared down at her.

She slid the Glock from her back waist holster and did as he ordered. Tommy picked it up and put it in his pocket.

"Walk towards the apartment building," Sidwell ordered.

She rose to her feet and as she walked, she watched the distance between them, waiting for her chance to do something to free herself. Tommy followed, his beefy thighs rubbing together and forcing his legs so far apart he waddled.

When they reached the building, Sidwell ordered her to follow the narrow path on its left. "Down there," he said. Cement steps led to what appeared to be a basement.

"No." She stopped.

"Go, or I'll shoot you here!"

"What difference would it make, here or down there? I'd be dead either way."

"I don't want to kill you, Inspector," Sidwell said in an eerily soft tone. "I simply need time to get away. I'm not a murderer, but I've made mistakes in my life, so I'm leaving. Now, go! If you want to live, listen to me!"

She could see no benefit to defying him further. Slowly, she walked down the steps.

He hung back, still not close enough for her to take him. "Open the door and walk to the far side of the room."

The door was unlocked. She played with thoughts of pulling the door shut behind her and locking it, but the paneling was so thin a bullet would easily penetrate it.

Inside, she saw that heating and ventilating systems for the building filled the bulk of the large space.

"Keep going. Move away from the door," he ordered. "I will shoot."

She heard his voice quaver nervously, and knew that was when people with guns were at their most dangerous.

As she crossed the room, she noticed some pipes on a table, and angled closer to them. Sidwell remained by the door. She had no idea if he was a good shot, but given his nervousness, the farther away he was, the more chance he would miss if he fired.

Still, she didn't relish testing his ability.

"Turn around!" he ordered.

She complied. "There's no need to do this, Mr. Sidwell. We can talk. Let me hear what your reasons are for all that has happened. Tell me what caused you so much trouble."

He scoffed. "Why should I bother?"

"If you had good reasons for whatever you did, you'll be helped. You and your attorney will be able to work something out, a plea deal. Maybe none of this was your fault, and you'll be let off altogether."

"It wasn't my fault! She was blackmailing me."

"Meaghan Bishop?" Rebecca asked.

"That's right. Everything was fine until she came back into my life. She met Pasternak—I have no idea when or where, but he's the one who told her about Big Caesar's and when she heard the owner was Harrison Sidwell, she knew that was my real name."

Rebecca found this confusing. "I take it she wasn't glad about that."

His face turned ugly. "She saw all that I have now, that I made something of myself. The bitch came on to me big time. I started seeing her again, bought her things. Clothes. I got her a nice place to live. I paid for everything. But she had changed. She did it to get even with me. I tried to break it off, and she threatened that if I didn't give her money every month, a lot of money, she would ruin me. I did some things in the past, bad things, that she knew about. She could send me to jail for years. I paid up as long as I could, doing everything I could think of to keep money coming in. But the more I tried, the worse everything turned. She ruined me! Everything I had worked for, everything I had, she destroyed!"

"There's your excuse," Rebecca said.

"I know what you're doing." He sneered at her. "I'm not stupid. It's not going to work. I'm out of here and no one will stop me."

"Why was Richie Amalfi involved?"

He stared at her with tired but venomous eyes, as if he had reached the end of his rope, and pondered whether to answer or to quickly end this and kill her. She held her breath. At this point, the pretentious but timid Harrison Sidwell had vanished completely, and in his place she saw the desperate low-life who once called himself Sonny Blakely. Finally, he said, "I heard the bitch and Pasternak talking. She didn't know I had bugged her place; she still never realized how smart I really am. Anyway, Pasternak told her about the loan Richie gave me. They decided that she should romance Richie. The fool thought she could hustle him, and that, when I lost the club, he'd sell it to her and Danny. I could have told her Richie's a lot smarter, and a lot better businessman than to fall for any of that."

And hopefully a better judge of character, Rebecca thought. But then, she remembered how stunned Richie had been at Sidwell's deceit, and also at the way Meaghan Bishop had played him. Maybe Richie was a more trusting person than he thought he was, especially to those people, like Sidwell, that he considered to be a friend. It wasn't a bad characteristic to have as far as she was concerned. "So what happened?" she asked Sidwell.

"I learned that she planned to meet Richie on Saturday. She'd get him to bring her to the club, let him see that she was friends with his good pal, Danny Pasternak. Then, she was going to do whatever it took to get good and close to him. She could have done it, too. Richie's got a soft side, a good heart. And she knows how to use a guy like that."

Rebecca suddenly found that she disliked Meaghan Bishop almost as much as Sidwell did. "I thought Danny Pasternak wasn't there Saturday night," she said.

He gave a cold, hard smile. "He wasn't. I told him we got a tip the police were going to raid the place looking for bookmaking. He split."

"But he wrote a note to Richie."

"No. He wrote a note to me some weeks earlier. It didn't have my name on it, just *'I need to see you now. Danny.'* For some reason I kept it. After I did away with Meaghan—and how surprised she was that I had the last laugh!—I put my plan in place. I picked up the shell from the bullet that killed her, and then, while Tommy delivered the note to Richie in a sealed envelope, I removed the gun's silencer and put in a magazine filled with only one bullet. Tommy hurried back to Danny's office where I gave him the gun, gloves, and a ski mask. All he had to do was get Richie to pull the trigger, aiming so that the blank went out the window. That was the diciest part of the whole operation. But Tommy's a strong guy, and the window in that room is big. He did it."

"But we found no second bullet," she said.

"That's because I watched from the back of the club while Tommy struggled with Richie so I could see where the bullet hit. I came back in to make sure the bouncers caught Richie and didn't let him go, then while everything was in chaos, I went out, removed the bullet from the wall of the building next door, then gouged and muddied it in a few spots."

"So that's why I didn't see you until late into the evening."

He shrugged. "I was a busy guy."

"Danny figured out that you were behind Meaghan's death, didn't he?" Rebecca said.

"Danny was on borrowed time, and he knew it. He was easy to ice. Richie, however, was a problem. When he escaped from you coppers, I worried how I'd get him, but Danny gave the answer there as well. I simply got word out to Danny's customers that Richie had all the information on their debts and gambling and he was going to make them pay him, or he'd go to the Feds with it. Rest assured that one of those guys—Reyes, Huang, somebody—will become nervous and get rid of him eventually. I'm surprised it hasn't happened yet. But it will. Now, I'm tired of all this talk! Tommy, get over here!"

"You won't get away with this Sidwell," Rebecca said. "Turn yourself in, explain that you were a victim, that you were being blackmailed and ruined by a vindictive woman you once loved. That should save you from murder one. But nothing will save you if you kill me. A cop killer gets a lethal injection in California. You don't want that."

Sidwell shook his head. "Inspector, stop. You have no proof. Without proof, I'm free. Tommy!"

The muscular giant lumbered closer. "Right here, boss."

"Shoot her."

Tommy lifted his gun, a cannon-like automatic, from his pocket, but kept it pointed at the ground. "You heard what she said, boss. If we kill a cop, it's gonna be tough to get away."

Sidwell pointed his gun at Tommy. "Do it."

"Don't listen to him, Tommy!" Rebecca cried as she stepped backwards, trying to increase the distance between her and the gun, looking for someplace to jump, to hide. "He just wants you to take the blame for everything. You can't trust him. He's gone after his friends, Danny and Richie, and even killed the woman he loved. He'll kill you, too, Tommy. You know it."

"She's lying," Sidwell said. "We're in this together, you and me. We trust each other."

Tommy gazed vacantly at Sidwell, blinked, then nodded. "Okay, boss," he mumbled as he raised his arm.

A shot went off and Tommy's gun flew into the air. Rebecca spun behind a furnace. Another shot hit Tommy in the knee and he crumbled.

Rebecca glanced towards Sidwell to see him turn and run for shelter. As Tommy crawled towards his gun, she lunged for a pipe, and hit him twice across the head and back, using all the strength she could muster. He fell flat, out cold. She scooped up his gun and dived behind some water heaters, all the while keeping an eye out for Sidwell.

The shots had come from a small window near the basement's ceiling. No one was there now. With Tommy's gun in hand, she crept along the room, trying to find where Sidwell hid.

The door to the basement lay open, and Sidwell was no longer in the room.

Richie appeared in the doorway. "Don't shoot, Rebecca! It's me."

She lowered the firearm.

He crossed the room to her in two long steps. "What the hell did they do to you?" He pushed her hair back and studied her face. "You're bleeding. Damn them! How do you feel? Let's get you to a hospital."

She stepped back and gingerly touched her forehead. Blood from a gash had run along her temple and cheek to her jacket. "I'll be okay. Just a little banged up." Tommy was still out as she cuffed him and retrieved her Glock from his pocket. "Let's get out of here. I may still be able to catch up to Sidwell."

"No way! You're hurt! Shay's gone after him. If anyone

can find him, Shay can. He'll let me know."

"Shay's here, too?" she said, and then realized he had to have been the sharp shooter who took out Tommy. "How did you find me?"

"Shay was watching Sidwell until you collected enough evidence to arrest him, and after you were followed the other day, and then everything else that was going on, I thought I'd better keep an eye on you. To our surprise, Shay and I both ended up at the same place. Now, I'm taking you home." He put his arm around her to help her up the stairs.

"No! When Tommy wakes up, he'll tell us everything. He's the first step in our proof of Sidwell's actions. I've got to call this in right now, and he needs medical help."

"So do you!"

"I'll be fine, really. I don't want you here when those squad cars and everyone else arrives."

"I'm no longer a suspect," he murmured as he ran his thumb along her forehead, wiping a rivulet of blood towards her temple so that it wouldn't drip into her eye, then his hand cupped her cheek. "I'm not leaving you alone."

His touch on her face was gentle, but she took hold of his wrist, stopping him. "Please. It's best if you aren't here. Believe me."

His eyes met hers a long moment, then he simply nodded.

She made the call. When she finished and turned his way once more, Richie was gone.

Chapter 20

WHILE REBECCA WAITED for an ambulance for Tommy, she contacted Sutter and told him what had happened, leaving off—at least for the moment—the part about Richie and Shay turning up to save her.

She knew she would have the problem of Tommy's version of events, but he probably didn't know where the shots had come from. She might even convince him that Sidwell shot him because he had hesitated to kill her. Tommy the hero. She shook her head.

Sidwell would cause her a similar problem when he got caught. He might well talk about the shots that were fired from the window.

She had no idea what she would say, and decided to cross that bridge when she came to it.

An entire cavalry of patrol cars converged on the scene as word of the shooting got out.

Tommy was just coming to as the ambulance arrived. He started to cry over the pain of the gunshot, and refused to speak as the EMTs helped him into the ambulance. Rebecca read him his rights, and then one of the patrol officers rode in the ambulance with Tommy as they took him to the hospital.

Rebecca refused any medical care beyond cleaning and bandaging the cuts and abrasions on her forehead. She also washed the blood from her face.

More than anything, she wanted to find Sidwell. Neither Richie nor Shay contacted her, making her believe Sidwell had somehow gotten past Shay and must be on the run.

Before leaving the area, she went into Sidwell's apartment and searched for anything that might give a hint of where he could be headed. She found nothing. Once more, she phoned Sutter who was already at the hospital waiting to question Tommy after the surgery to remove the bullet in his knee. She asked him to meet her at Big Caesar's. Perhaps more information could be found there.

As usual, she arrived at the nightclub before Sutter did.

She decided not to wait for him. The club wasn't open to the public yet, but she knocked and a waitress opened the door.

"I need to see Sidwell's office." Rebecca showed her badge and pushed her way inside.

"I don't think he's here yet. I haven't seen him," the waitress said.

"Stay out of the way." Rebecca drew her gun and marched down the hall, the waitress running along beside her.

"You can't go in there," the waitress cried, but stopped in her tracks at the hard, ice-cold stare Rebecca cast her way.

Rebecca followed procedure by knocking on Sidwell's door and announcing, "Police. Open up." As expected, no one answered.

She opened the door.

Sidwell sat slumped in the chair behind his desk, a bullet hole in his temple. She ran to him and tried to find a pulse. She couldn't. The body was already turning cold.

A gun with a silencer lay on the floor below his right hand.

A note was on his desk:

I can't go on without Meaghan. I'm sorry for all I've done.

Sonny

It looked like suicide, but why, Rebecca wondered, would he have used a silencer? Why would he care if anyone heard his gun go off?

She saw a number of handwritten notes on Sidwell's calendar, and a few sticky notes on his computer. The handwriting on the suicide note matched all the others.

Rebecca looked up to see the waitress standing frozen in the doorway, her eyes enormous.

"Did you see anyone come in here?" Rebecca asked.

She shook her head.

"Are you sure you didn't see Mr. Sidwell enter the club?"

"I didn't," she whispered.

"Did you see any strangers in here?"

Again, the waitress shook her head.

Rebecca made the necessary phone calls to get the Medical Examiner and Crime Scene Investigation to the scene, and then interviewed the rest of the staff. All gave her the exact same answers as the waitress.

Rebecca spent the rest of the day and long into the night in Homicide, completing paperwork on Tommy's arrest, and answering questions, written and oral, about everything that had happened between her and Sidwell before he ran off, and then later, when she found him in his office.

When she finally got to go home, she found her apartment empty except for Spike. She thought Richie might have been there to celebrate solving the murders. She thought she might have received at least a phone call.

Instead, there was nothing.

She went to bed and for the first time in a week, she should have slept well. For some reason, she didn't.

The next morning, she watched the medical examiner perform an autopsy on Sidwell's body.

"The only finding at all strange is he did have a smashed knuckle on the pinky finger of his left hand. But that sort of thing could happen for any number of reasons. It isn't enough to affect my conclusion. I'm finding that this man committed suicide," Evelyn Ramirez said as she finished up. She gazed at Rebecca. "I have the feeling that isn't what you wanted to hear."

"No, it's fine," Rebecca said. "It's just that I've never heard of a suicide using a silencer. Most wouldn't care about the noise, and it makes the gun more awkward to handle."

Ramirez shrugged. "A guy has to be nuts to kill himself to begin with. A silencer is one of the least strange things I've seen a person use."

"I guess so," Rebecca said, reminding herself that everything pointed towards suicide, including Sidwell's note, and no physical evidence contradicted that finding. She thanked the ME, who would soon submit a written report on the autopsy.

Back at her desk, she matched withdrawals from Sidwell's bank account to deposits into Meaghan Bishop's account.

She worked on the report about the two murders. It was

going to be long and complicated, and would take some time to complete. She also, finally, finished up the report on the murder of the poor liquor store clerk from last Friday night. She found it hard to think that case had happened barely a week ago; it seemed more like an eternity had passed.

Going home to her apartment that night, once again, only Spike greeted her, and damned if he didn't seem to be looking for Richie. She took him out to the yard and sat to watch him play.

Kiki came down the backstairs to join her. "Hey, Becca! How you doin'?"

"Okay."

Kiki sat on the bench at her side. "So, how's it going with Casanova?"

Rebecca shook her head. "It isn't. It was never that way between us. The case is over. He's already gone his way, and I'm going mine."

"Oh well," Kiki said with a heavy sigh, "don't worry about it. There's a lot more fish in the sea."

"Right," Rebecca agreed. Kiki's cliché made her think of another one that she had heard this past week, "A leopard doesn't change its spots." That pretty much summed up Richie.

The next day at work, she received a call that the police found an abandoned black Buick that not only had been reported stolen days earlier, but also matched the description of the car people saw in the vicinity at the time of Danny Pasternak's drive-by shooting.

She went with the Crime Scene techs to check it out. Harrison Sidwell's fingerprints were found on the steering wheel and driver's door handle.

Later, at her desk, she finally finished the report that presented her conclusions on the murders of Meaghan Bishop and Daniel Pasternak. All she had left to do was to sign it.

Sidwell was clearly guilty. He admitted killing Meaghan Bishop and Danny Pasternak, yet the whole business of his suicide continued to nag at her. It allowed the case to end almost too neatly in one, big, all-the-i's-dotted-and-t's-crossed package.

She couldn't stop her mind from replaying, over and over, Richie's words after he stopped Tommy from killing her. He said Shay had gone after Sidwell, and if anyone could find him, Shay could.

She believed it.

Sidwell had been a clever man. He had been meticulous in so much that he had done, the scamming, gambling, even keeping a blackmailer in check for quite a few months, that it seemed odd for him to make such a bonehead error as to leave his fingerprints on the car he drove to kill Pasternak, and to abandon it on a street in the city where it was sure to be found.

Maybe he hadn't abandoned it there. Maybe someone got him to tell where he'd hidden it and then moved it to a spot where the police were sure to find it.

And why did Sidwell go back to his office after the shoot-out? Why not run?

Unless—she shuddered—in all of this, he had no choice. If Shay had found him, she doubted Shay was big on options.

Rebecca gave up. She had to stop fighting her report's findings. She had no definitive reason to hold off concluding the case. It was neat, no loose ends, and perhaps a tad too tidy, but if everyone was buying it, who was she among so many?

Case solved. Score one for the team.

Finally, she signed her report and dropped it on Lt. Eastwood's desk. Before leaving work, she called the burner phone number Richie had used.

"This is Rebecca. I just wanted to let you know that all charges against you have been dropped. The case is over, all wrapped up, finished. You don't have to worry about it anymore." She drew in her breath. "I hope everything is okay. I guess that's it. Good-bye."

She hung up. It seemed there should have been more to say.

But why? What?

She put on her jacket and left the office. She would stop at McDonald's on the way home. They were running a two dollar special on Quarter Pounders.

Somewhere, Glickman was smiling.

Chapter 21

B IG CAESAR'S? ARE YOU kidding me? Did you know I just had a case there?" Rebecca said to her date as she settled into his green Honda Civic.

Officer Tristan Davis had recently graduated from Officer Training School and had been assigned to the Taravel station. Rebecca met him when she gave police cadets a tour of the Bureau of Inspectors, and she couldn't help but notice the tall, sandy-haired, hazel-eyed officer. He was about thirty, and this was his first job since leaving the Marines. To her pleasant surprise, two weeks later, he phoned her at work and asked her out. Of course, she said yes. He was her kind of guy.

"I thought you would enjoy seeing it as a customer instead of as a detective. I mean, you will enjoy it, won't you? Wasn't it some time ago that the murders happened?"

"About a month," she said. Actually, thirty-seven days had passed since she'd found Sidwell's body.

"They're running some sort of reopening special, and I have tickets for the cover charge and two drinks each—which is my limit, anyway." He smiled, apparently thrilled to be getting into the place without charge. Clearly, he was new to police work.

His face fell when she said nothing. "If you don't want to go ..."

If she didn't, she realized he would be on the spot to figure out where to take her instead. Any place else she suggested in this city would be expensive, and it would be a shame to waste complimentary tickets.

He had warned her that she should dress up, that they were going someplace "really nice," and she had done so. Her form-fitting shimmery emerald green dress was sleeveless and cut low in front and back, and she wore her hair with a side part, falling soft and sleek down past her shoulders.

"It's fine," she said with a smile. "I'm sure it'll seem quite different from the last time I was there." Talk about an understatement, she thought.

They parked in a lot around the corner from the club. That fee alone would cost Tristan quite a chunk of change.

The inside of the club was freshly painted, but not much else had changed. She didn't recognize any of the help. Tristan turned over the tickets and they were shown to seats surprisingly near the band. As in the past, big-band songs were being played. She would have thought such music would only appeal to an older, if not old, clientele, but a large number of thirty-somethings were there, probably enjoying the chance to dress, dine, and dance elegantly.

They ordered drinks, and as the band played *"Embraceable You,"* Tristan asked Rebecca to dance. He was a bit awkward and explained that really wasn't his style of dancing. He was more a Nine-Inch Nails kind of guy. She wanted to ask why, in that case, had he brought her here, but decided that might sound bitchy, and he was much too nice for that.

Still, he was clearly glad when the music ended and they

could sit. A tray of appetizers with shrimp, prawns, and lobster appeared at their table, compliments of the house.

They talked about work. He was quite interested in her career and how she rose through the ranks. She found him to be a pleasant, handsome, clearly good-hearted fellow who wore his ambition on his sleeve. She reminded herself that she was most likely that way when she started out in police work. He seemed to be of the "it's not what you do, but who you know" school. The unkind thought crossed her mind that their date might soon be over if she told him that knowing her would be of no use whatsoever to his career.

The more Tristan talked, the more she realized the only thing they had in common was work. Much as she had hoped otherwise, that hardly made for a scintillating date. She kept trying her best to smile.

She was studying the appetizer tray and had just reached for a scallop, when a familiar voice said, "Welcome to my club."

Her fork poised in mid-air as she looked up. Her mouth dropped. Forget *The Godfather*, tonight he was pure James Bond, debonair in a black tuxedo jacket with a bowtie and even a small red boutonniere in the lapel. "Richie?"

He grinned at her reaction. "Rebecca," he said, giving a slight bow, and then reached across the table to shake hands with her date. "Tristan, so glad you could make it."

Tristan jumped to his feet. "Thank you for the tickets, Mr. Amalfi. Your club is beautiful!"

"Are you being treated well?" he asked, facing Rebecca.

"Yes, very much so," Tristan answered. "The appetizers are delicious."

"Rebecca?" Richie asked.

"Everything he said," she answered.

Richie studied her a moment. "You look beautiful

tonight."

He had never said anything like that to her, and it took her aback. She reminded herself of how much he irked her at times, and that there was no reason she should feel tongue-tied or as if she had butterflies in her stomach just because he was all dressed up. Clothes, as they said, obviously made the man.

She wasn't able to stop her frown. "Thank you."

"So," Tristan, still standing, turned to Rebecca. "Mr. Amalfi suggested I not tell you that we were coming here tonight, that it would be more fun to surprise you after all you two had been through trying to find the guy who murdered someone here."

"Oh?" Rebecca didn't like the tone of that.

Richie tugged at his ear lobe as he glanced at the nearby customers. "Yeah, well, let's keep it down. I don't like reminding people of all that, you know?"

Tristan's eyebrows lifted. "Oh, sorry! I should have realized..."

"Mr. Amalfi also doesn't like to be reminded of it"—Rebecca folded her arms and met his gaze—"since he was the prime suspect."

"Really?" Tristan asked.

"Yes." She never glanced Tristan's way. "I even arrested him."

Richie glared at her.

She glared back.

Tristan's eyes widened as they leaped from one to the other. "Oh."

"Sit," Richie told him, his voice gruff. "I didn't mean to disturb you." He gave a nod of good-bye and turned away.

As Tristan dropped into his chair, the band began to play *"Arrivederci Roma."*

Richie glanced back at Rebecca, and saw that she was still watching him. He strolled back to her. "An old Italian love song, made for dancing." He held out his hand, his head ever so slightly cocked. "Inspector?"

She would have gladly refused, but his tone said he expected her to say "No," and even his eyes had a glint of something mocking. She took the napkin off her lap, plopped it on the table and stood. "Sure."

Surprise flashed across his face, then vanished. He led her far from the table before he took her in his arms.

The scent of his after shave brought back memories of when he was all but living at her house. Memories that were surprisingly good, and even bizarrely fun. Memories that she didn't want to have.

They danced in silence a moment, then he asked, "How have you been, Rebecca?"

"All is well. I suspect you got my message."

"About the case, yes," he said. "I would have called back, but I didn't want to impose."

"There was no need to," she said quickly.

"Right."

After listening to a few more bars of the song, she said, "So, tell me, how did you get all this?"

He looked around the room, all the people, the band, the food, and seemed both pleased and perhaps a little overwhelmed. Somehow, that reminded her of when he was a part of her life, not so cocky, not so self-assured. Damn, if she didn't miss that fellow. "Turns out my loan covered the down payment plus," he said. "And you know this place makes money if run right."

"So now you're a nightclub owner," she said with a smile. "Who would have thought it?"

"Not you," he said softly.

"You should have called and told me about it."

"What, so I could listen to you hang up on me?"

That hurt. "I might not have," she said quietly.

"Oh? I know you don't think much of me."

"That's not true," she said, then thought about it. Thought of her suspicions about Sidwell's suicide, of the evidence that fell too neatly into place. "I mean..."

"I know," he said, then didn't speak for a long while as they slowly spun in time with the music to the far side of the dance floor. He danced very well, she thought. The music continued and became a medley of popular Italian songs. Dean Martin would have been proud.

She felt herself relaxing a bit. She knew Richie read her far too well. She didn't trust him, didn't particularly like him, but for some reason, being with him, even dancing with him, felt right. She listened to the music.

He caught her eye. "It seems someone asked Tristan to leave. I guess you're stuck with me the rest of the evening."

"What?" She looked across the floor, but her table was now empty. "He wouldn't have just gone off like that. What did they say to him?"

Still holding her gaze, he raised his chin ever so slightly. "Maybe that there was something going on at the station and he was needed. Or maybe that the lady was otherwise occupied tonight."

She all but gasped. "That was arrogant!"

"Were you having such a great time?" he asked.

She hesitated, then admitted, "Not so much."

"Good! I thought you looked a little bored."

She smiled, but also shook her head. He was beyond arrogant. But then the smile vanished and she paled. "Wait a minute, did you tell him to ask me out?"

He grinned. "Hell, no! It was the talk of the Taravel

station, so I heard, that from the time he met you the kid was head-over-heels. Puppy love, I think they call it. I decided to give him a break and suggested a woman like you should be brought someplace with class, somewhere like this club."

"You're terrible."

"I know."

"He was a Marine!"

"That I didn't know. You want me to call him back?"

She didn't need to think about it, but answered simply and honestly, "No."

"Good," he murmured.

"Come Back to Sorrento" ended and *"Al Di La"* began.

She had loved the song since she was a young teenager and went to a dance at the middle school gym. For some reason, instead of only fast songs, the older tune played— probably some teacher's favorite—and she danced it with the boy she was crazy about at the time. Unfortunately, kshe never danced with him again.

"This is one of my favorite songs," she said, a bit wistfully.

He caught her gaze. "Mine, too. But the way they translate it is all wrong. It's hard to translate, but it means something like 'more than that,' 'even more,' 'beyond.' Something like that."

"You understand the words?"

"Sure. He's telling her how much she means to him, his love, his feelings." His voice turned low and soft as he continued. "The end is the best, when he says even more than infinite time, even more than life...*al di la, ci sei tu per me*...more than that, that's what you are for me."

Her breath caught even as she reminded herself that he was only translating words to the song. "That's very pretty," she said trying, for some reason, not to look at him. "A lovely song."

"A song...yes, it is," he said, then turned her round and round as they continued to dance.

Despite herself, she felt her spirits lift, found herself relieved that he'd sent Tristan home, and unexpectedly glad to be with him again.

She smiled, enjoying the feel of his arms around her, the sound of his voice, the touch of his hands. And as they danced, she stepped just a little bit closer.

Find out what happens next in
the lives of
Rebecca & Richie in:

TWO O'CLOCK HEIST

June, 2014

~ ~ ~ ~ ~

Rebecca & Richie meet and share
their first mystery/adventure
in the novella:

THE THIRTEENTH SANTA

Both stories brought to you by
QUAIL HILL PRESS

About the Author

Joanne Pence was born and raised in northern California, and now makes her home in Idaho. She has been an award-winning, *USA Today* best-selling author of mysteries, and has also written suspense, historical fiction, contemporary romance, romantic suspense, and fantasy.

Joanne hopes you'll enjoy her books, which present a variety of times, places, and reading experiences, from mysterious to thrilling, emotional to lightly humorous, as well as powerful tales of times long past.

Visit her at www.joannepence.com.

Ancient Echoes

Over two hundred years ago, a covert expedition shadowing Lewis and Clark disappeared in the wilderness of Central Idaho. Now, seven anthropology students and their professor vanish in the same area. The key to finding them lies in an ancient secret, one that men throughout history have sought to unveil.

Michael Rempart is a brilliant archeologist with a colorful and controversial career, but he is plagued by a sense of the supernatural and a spiritual intuitiveness. Joining Michael are a CIA consultant on paranormal phenomena, a washed-up local sheriff, and a former scholar of Egyptology. All must overcome their personal demons as they attempt to save the students and learn the expedition's terrible secret.

Seems Like Old Times

When Lee Reynolds, nationally known television news anchor, returns to the small town where she was born to sell her now-vacant childhood home, little does she expect to find that her first love has moved back to town. Nor does she expect that her feelings for him are still so strong.

Tony Santos had been a major league baseball player, but now finds his days of glory gone. He's gone back home to raise his young son as a single dad.

Both Tony and Lee have changed a lot. Yet, being with him, she finds that in her heart, it seems like old times...

Dance With A Gunfighter

Gabriella Devere wants vengeance. She grows up quickly when she witnesses the murder of her family by a gang of outlaws, and vows to make them pay for their crime. When the law won't help her, she takes matters into her own hands.

Jess McLowry left his war-torn Southern home to head West, where he hired out his gun. When he learns what happened to Gabriella's family, and what she plans, he knows a young woman like her will have no chance against the outlaws, and vows to save her the way he couldn't save his own family.

But the price of vengeance is high and Gabriella's willingness to sacrifice everything ultimately leads to the book's deadly and startling conclusion.

This harsh and gritty tale of the old West was named a finalist for the Willa Cather Literary Award in Historical Fiction.

The Ghost of Squire House

For decades, the home built by reclusive artist, Paul Squire, has stood empty on a windswept cliff overlooking the ocean. Those who attempted to live in the home soon fled in terror. Jennifer Barrett knows nothing of the history of the house she inherited. All she knows is she's glad for the chance to make a new life for herself.

It's Paul Squire's duty to rid his home of intruders, but something about this latest newcomer's vulnerable status...and resemblance of someone from his past...dulls his resolve. Jennifer would like to find a real flesh-and-blood man to liven her days and nights—someone to share her life with—but living in the artist's house, studying his paintings, she is surprised at how close she feels to him.

A compelling, prickly ghost with a tortured, guilt-ridden past, and a lonely heroine determined to start fresh, find themselves in a battle of wills and emotion in this ghostly fantasy of love, time, and chance.

Gold Mountain

Against the background of San Francisco at the time of the Great Earthquake and Fire of 1906 comes a tale of love and loss. Ruth Greer, wealthy daughter of a shipping magnate, finds a young boy who has run away from his home in Chinatown—an area of gambling parlors, opium dens, sing-song girls, as well as families trying to eke out a living. It is also home to a number of highbinder tongs, the infamous "hatchet men" of Chinese lore.

There, Ruth meets the boy's father, Li Han-lin, the handsome, enigmatic leader of one such tong, and discovers he is neither as frightening, cruel, or wanton as reputation would have her believe. As Ruth's fascination with the area grows, she finds herself pulled deeper into the intrigue of the lawless area, and Han-lin's life. But the two are from completely different worlds, and when both worlds are shattered by the earthquake and fire that destroys San Francisco, they face their ultimate test.

Dangerous Journey

C.J. Perkins is trying to find her brother who went missing while on a Peace Corps assignment in Asia. All she knows is that the disappearance has something to do with a "White Dragon." Darius Kane, adventurer and bounty hunter, seems to be her only hope, and she practically shanghais him into helping her.

With a touch of the romantic adventure film Romancing the Stone, C.J. and Darius follow a trail that takes them through the narrow streets of Hong Kong, the backrooms of San Francisco's Chinatown, and the wild jungles of Borneo as they pursue both her brother and the White Dragon. The closer C.J. gets to them, the more danger she finds herself in—and it's not just danger of losing her life, but also of losing her heart.

[This is a completely revised author's edition of novel previously published as *Armed and Dangerous*.]

The Angie Amalfi Mysteries

Gourmet cook, sometime food columnist, sometime restaurant critic, and generally "underemployed" person Angelina Amalfi burst upon the mystery scene in SOMETHING'S COOKING, in which she met San Francisco Homicide Inspector Paavo Smith. Since that time—over the course of 15 books and a novella—she's wanted two things in life, a good job...and Paavo.

Here's a brief outline of each book in the order written:

Something's Cooking

For sassy and single food writer Angie Amalfi, life's a banquet—until the man who's been contributing unusual recipes for her food column is found dead. But Angie is hardly one to simper in fear—so instead she simmers over the delectable homicide detective assigned to the case.

Too Many Cooks

In TOO MANY COOKS, Angie's talked her way into a job on a pompous, third-rate chef's radio call-in show. But when a successful and much envied restaurateur is poisoned, Angie finds the case far more interesting than trying to make her pretentious boss sound good.

Cooking Up Trouble

Angie Amalfi's latest job, developing the menu for a new inn, sounds enticing—especially since it means spending a week in scenic Northern California with her homicide-detective boyfriend. But once she arrives at the soon-to-be-opened Hill Haven Inn, she's not so sure anymore. The added ingredients of an ominous treat, a missing person, and a woman making eyes at her man leave Angie convinced that the only recipe in this inn's kitchen is one for disaster.

Cooking Most Deadly

Food columnist Angie Amalfi has it all. But while she's wondering if it's time to cut the wedding cake with her boyfriend, Paavo, he becomes obsessed with a grisly homicide that has claimed two female victims. Angie becomes the next target of a vendetta that stretches from the dining rooms of San Francisco's elite to the seedy Tenderloin.

Cook's Night Out

Angie has decided to make her culinary name by creating the perfect chocolate confection: angelinas. Donating her delicious rejects to a local mission, Angie soon finds that the mission harbors more than the needy, and to save not only her life, but Paavo's as well, she's going to have to discover the truth faster than you can beat egg whites to a peak.

Cooks Overboard

Angie Amalfi's long-awaited vacation with her detective boyfriend has all the ingredients of a romantic getaway—a sail to Acapulco aboard a freighter, no crowds, no Homicide Department worries, and a red bikini. But it isn't long before Angie's *Love Boat* fantasies are headed for stormy seas—the cook tries to jump off the ship, Paavo is acting mighty strange, and someone's added murder to the menu...

A Cook In Time

Angie Amalfi has a way with food and people, but her newest business idea is turning out to be shakier than a fruit-filled gelatin mold. Now, her first—and only—clients for "Fantasy Dinners" are none other than a group of UFO chasers and government conspiracy fanatics. But when it seems that the group has a hidden agenda greater than anything on the *X-Files*, Angie's determined to find out the truth before it takes her out of this world...for good.

To Catch A Cook

Between her latest "sure-fire" foray into the food industry—video restaurant reviews—and her concern over Paavo's depressed state, Angie's plate is full to overflowing. Paavo has never come to terms with the fact that his mother abandoned him when he was four, leaving behind only a mysterious present. But when the token disappears, Angie discovers a lethal goulash of intrigue, betrayal, and mayhem that may spell disaster for her and Paavo.

Bell, Cook, and Candle

For once, Angie's newest culinary venture, "Comical Cakes," seems to be a roaring success! But there's nothing funny about her boyfriend Paavo's latest case—a series of baffling murders that may be rooted in satanic ritual. And it gets harder to focus on pastry alone when strange "accidents" and desecrations to her baked creations begin occurring with frightening regularity—leaving Angie to wonder whether she may end up as devil's food of a different kind.

If Cooks Could Kill

Angie Amalfi's culinary adventures always seem to fall flat, so now she's decided to cook up something different: love. But her earnest attempts at matchmaking don't go so well—her friend Connie is stood up by a no-show jock. Now Connie's fallen for a tarnished loner, and soon finds herself in the middle of a murder investigation. Angie's determined to find the real killer, but when the trail leads to the kitchen of her favorite restaurant, she fears she's about to discover a family recipe that dishes out disaster...and murder!

Two Cooks A-Killing

Angie hates to leave the side of her hunky fiancé, Paavo, but she gets an offer she can't refuse. She'll be preparing the banquet for her favorite soap opera's reunion special, on the estate where the show was originally filmed! But when a corpse turns up in the mansion's cellar, and Angie starts snooping around to investigate a past on-set death, she discovers that real-life events may be even more theatrical than the soap's on-screen drama.

Courting Disaster

Against her instincts, Angie agrees to let her control-freak mother plan her engagement party—she's just too busy to do it herself. And Angie's even more swamped when murder enters the picture. Now she must follow the trail of a mysterious pregnant kitchen helper at a nearby Greek eatery—a woman who her friendly neighbor Stan is infatuated with. And when Angie gets a little too close to the action, it looks like her fiancé Paavo may end up celebrating solo, after the untimely d.o.a. of his hapless fiancé!

Red Hot Murder

Angie and Paavo have had enough familial input regarding their upcoming wedding to last a lifetime. So Angie leaps at the chance to spend some time with her fiancé in a sun-drenched Arizona town. But when a wealthy local is murdered, uncovering a hotbed of deadly town secrets, Angie's getaway with her lover is starting to look more and more like her final meal.

The DaVinci Cook

Just when dilettante chef Angie Amalfi's checkered culinary career seems to be looking up, she has to drop everything and hightail it to Rome. Her realtor sister is in a stew—accused of murder. To make matters worse, a priceless religious relic is missing as well—so the Amalfi girls are joining forces in the Eternal City...and diving head-first into a simmering cauldron of big trouble.

Cooking Spirits

Culinary queen Angie Amalfi has put aside her gourmet utensils to concentrate on her upcoming wedding, but instead of the answer to her heart's desires, she scrambles to deal with wedding planners with bizarre ideas, wedding dresses that don't flatter, squabbling relatives, and worries over where she and Paavo will live after the wedding. But all of that pales when Angie finds the perfect house for them, except for one little problem—the house may be haunted.

oOo

10459634R00139

Made in the USA
San Bernardino, CA
16 April 2014